Down To Business

D1521801

J. K. Holiday

ISBN: **1540435083**
ISBN 13: **9781540435088**
Library of Congress Control Number: **2016959907**
CreateSpace Independent Publishing Platform
North Charleston, South Carolina

1

Extreme Networking

Conference days wore on me like control-top panty hose. I could only take notes on a pad in my lap in a gold-on-gold ballroom for so long. This was the last session, and it was almost over. I wanted to duck out early, but Bob, who worked for another member of the Alliance, said he wanted to talk to me after the session.

"I only have time for one more question," the speaker said. Thank fucking God. Of course, a hand shot up.

"Can you explain..."

Shut up. Shut *up*! I felt a tap on my shoulder. I turned around. Bob, brown-bearded, bespectacled, and a little disheveled—the archetype of Boomer activists—stretching his lanky body forward on his chair, notes in hand, motioned that we should go. God bless you, Bob.

"What's up?" I asked as the heavy oak door closed behind us, making a resonant thump.

"What are you doing for dinner? My boss wants me to take some people out." Bob represented ethanol, by far the most widely used renewable fuel and definitely the most envied. While other energy technologies lobbied hard for their position in the market, ethanol was already required in all clean gasoline. To make it even less popular, it used to be federally subsidized to the tune of fifty cents per gallon. Ethanol comes mostly from corn, so it had always had the support of the farm lobby as well as its fuel-specific activists. Bob's boss was making sure that ethanol still had some friends.

"I don't have any plans. I'd love to go."

"OK, meet me in the lobby at six thirty. I've got to go invite some other people."

"Sure, see you then." Sweet. It was always fun to go out with a bunch of people at a conference—plus the host would always pay for alcohol. Not so with my expensed meals. I went upstairs to change out of my suit. We were a casual office, so conferences were one of the few occasions I wore panty hose.

I pulled on black pants with a sweetheart-cut, pink silk cardigan. The summer sweater was snug on my boobs, without showing cleavage. It showed a shadow of my black lace bra underneath, but I could get away with it. I drew on some brown eyeliner, which I'd just bought to match my eyes. I changed my lipstick to hot pink to match my sweater and fluffed my hair. I examined my new hair color and wondered if "Light Brown Sugar" clashed with my olive complexion. Maybe, but at least it covered the grays; thirty-two was way too young to go salt-and-pepper. I noticed a tan on my face from the conference, just from standing outside between sessions. I spritzed some perfume and headed out. As I walked out of the elevator bank, I took in the cheery Pacific-themed lobby that had fish murals, furniture and paint in shades of aqua, porthole-style windows, and a huge underwater scene etched into the all-glass front wall. Just then I saw the back of Bob's wavy brown head. He was talking to a group of people by the big aquarium in the atrium lounge. I knew most of them, and the others looked familiar. Environmental circles don't have big circumferences.

"Hey, Angie. We're just waiting for two more people," Bob said, bringing me into the circle. He gestured to a portion of the group I'd already met. "You know these ladies and gentlemen, and this is Sophie

Black from Environmental Research Alliance. Angie's a director at Hydrogen Futures." I reached out and shook her hand as Bob continued speaking. "And Nick Martone from the Green Fund."

Oh my God, Nick Martone. The hottest guy in energy and a legendary player. Dark brown hair, bright green eyes, long eyelashes, full lips, goatee. Man, did he fill out a suit! I could almost see the cuts in his arms through it. His adult cartoon mosaic tie hung flat—no extra pounds on that guy.

He smiled and reached out his hand. "Angie, I read your article in *Fuels Today*. I loved your take on diversifying funding. It's a real common-sense approach."

Wow, he even made business speak sexy. More importantly, he read *my* article? He remembered *my* name? Nobody ever looks at bylines in magazines. I couldn't believe it. Nick Martone, environmental rock star, thought *my* position was innovative? I'd seen him around but never met him. He was even better looking up close. I willed my hand not to sweat as I shook his.

He had the perfect handshake—firm, confident, and focused. "I'd love to talk some more about it," he said.

"Sure," I replied.

Great answer, Angie, I thought. I meet Nick Martone, and I'm rendered monosyllabic. I wasn't usually like this, but I'd admired him from afar for a long time. All the single "Green Girls" in our circles did. I wondered how many syllables I'd need to seduce him. Not many, based on the women I'd seen him with. Uh-huh. As if players went for smart girls, heavy on the curves. Well, good eye candy for dinner, anyway. And no extra calories.

Bob pulled me out of my little world. "This is Angie Pappas." I turned away from Nick and extended my hand to a silver-haired guy. His name didn't register. I was still thinking about Nick Martone. "And it looks like everybody's here. Let's go get a couple of cabs."

Silver Hair chatted me up as we went out the door. He was new to the energy lobby. According to him, he was a big deal in his previous field, preserving green spaces. The first cab came, a sedan, and half of the group got in. Silver Hair continued to ask me all kinds of questions about hydrogen as we waited for the next cab. Nick was talking to Sophie and another woman whose name I forgot.

It took a while, but the second cab finally came, also a sedan. Honestly, when you call a cab for nine people, the company should know to send a van. Silver Hair headed toward it as Nick swept in front of us, opened the door, gestured with his arm, and said, "After you, miss." He slid in next to me.

Silver Hair let his colleague sit on my other side and negotiated with the other woman to move from front to back. She acquiesced. She was tiny and probably used to those requests. God knows nobody ever asked me to squeeze in like that. But any four adults in the back of a cab was gonna be tight. And Nick Martone's Lauder-for-Men-scented body was pressed against mine. How was it possible he wore my favorite cologne? "I hope you don't mind," he said as he draped his arm across the worn gray pleather seat behind me.

"Oh, no, it's fine," I said, beginning to sweat. His warm body pressed against my side. I rested my arm on my knee to make room. No, I didn't mind at all. Silver Hair told the driver where to go, and we were on our way.

"I know we just met, but I feel so...so close," Nick teased, as cityscapes became vineyards as we got closer to wine country. It was supposed to be a destination restaurant with a huge wine list, overlooking a sea of vines.

"That's funny; I feel really close to you right now, too," I said. Two syllables. Nice. But funny. Points for funny, right?

He laughed. "We got interrupted before. I really liked what you said about the approach to funding in that article. Everybody's vying for more support, especially mine, because the whole funding thing is in the wrong hands in Congress. I liked what you said about tying environmental funding to the committees who know more about the technologies."

What people outside the beltway failed to realize was that DC wasn't about ideals or laws; it was about money. When the president championed an industry, that meant subsidies. When we lobbied Congress to level the playing field with Big Oil, we were asking for favorable laws for our industry, yes, but we were also asking for funding or tax credits. Since it was the nascent industries that received the bulk of the money, we nonprofits all vied for grants and research contracts to pay our bills.

Nick ran a nonprofit that funded other nonprofits, sort of a UNICEF for the environmental world. His organization raised and invested money now, but there was lots of speculation about where the seed money came from. Most people thought it was family money, because how could a guy who rode whaleboats for Greenpeace after college fund a financial organization? Others thought he attracted a huge seed grant from a Cornell buddy's family. Cornell also sparked some debate. Did he go as a regular student or on scholarship? He was definitely smart enough for a free ride. The thing was, he was cagey about his family. He was from Jersey, and Martone was a pretty common name there, so nobody really knew anything about his family.

"Yeah, the problem is there's one big pot—well, not big enough if you ask me, but the people allocating the money are congressional bean counters. They don't know enough about how to help develop the technologies. If you put the money in the hands of members who are more familiar with them, the money will go a lot farther."

"And that contributes to all the competition among technologies. You know I see you all here, and you all know each other, and you're all friendly, but when I read proposals, the gloves are off. You name names and take no prisoners."

"Money's money. Doesn't matter what your intentions are; when it comes to money, it's dog-eat-dog." I drew in a breath. Man, his cologne smelled good.

"Don't I know it. I could live without the negativity I see so much. So, what exactly is your position over at Hydrogen Futures?"

"I do research, lobbying, and I write targeted articles for industry and laymen's pubs. It's public relations, really, but no one calls it that. They call me a director, but there are only six of us, so everybody's a director."

When we pulled up to the restaurant, Nick got out and held up his hand. "May I offer you a hand, miss?" He winked.

I took his hand and smiled. "Thank you, sir." Was he flirting? With me? God, I needed a drink.

Silver Hair cornered him on the way into the restaurant. On the way to the cab, Silver Hair had mentioned to me that his nonprofit had just applied for a grant from Nick's nonprofit. Taking my fill of the grapevines, I followed them in.

The restaurant was decorated with vineyard scenes with fake grape trellises above. Everybody from the first cab was seated at a round table. The first thing I noticed was that it held four bottles of wine. Thank God. I went toward Bob. Nick practically ran around the other side of the table, situated himself between Bob and me, and held my chair. Then he sat between us. What was going on here?

"White or red?" Bob asked.

"White." The whole bottle. Please.

Bob passed the white to Nick, who poured me a glass. I grabbed the glass and took the biggest sip I could. You just can't chug wine. Nick continued our private conversation through most of dinner, interrupted only by direct questions from other people in our party. I calmed down after the first glass of wine, and after the second, he'd brushed his hand against my leg a few times. Each brush was a new experience of electricity coursing through my body. Damn, was I gonna get a piece of that? I poured myself another glass of wine. By the time we left, or rather Nick solicitously ushered me out, I thought it might actually happen. When the second cab came and he told the others to go ahead—we'd wait—I was sure of it.

Finally in our own cab, he asked me where I was from. "New York," I replied.

"We got a problem here; I'm from New Jersey."

"Uh-oh."

He leaned in. Close. Lowered his voice. "Maybe we can make an arrangement."

Those soft lips touched mine. I let out an involuntary squeak as a tingle shot straight to my crotch. Smooth, Angie, smooth.

After the kiss, I struggled for words. "Maybe we can."

He kissed me again. Oh my God, those lips went on forever! Then he parted his lips, explored my tongue, and sucked it a little. No one had done that since high school, and with that visceral memory, my whole lower half shivered. Our tongues played and wrestled, and by the time we'd got to the hotel, his hand was on my back under my sweater, pulling me closer. How'd he get under my sweater? Didn't matter. I wanted to feel more skin on skin.

He paid the cabbie. "Wait here," he said as he got out of the car. He appeared at my door and opened it for me, hand outstretched. "Miss?"

I knew he was charming. "Thank you." I took his hand as I got out of the cab. He didn't let go as we walked into the hotel. Weird. I told myself that he treated all of his women this way, but everyone we knew was staying at the hotel, and I expected him to be more discreet. I didn't say anything about it and mess up my shot with him.

"Would you like to come up?" he said at the elevator.

Does a shark shit in the ocean? I couldn't think of anything I wanted more. I smiled. "Yes." I couldn't wait to see what was under that suit.

In the elevator, he pushed me up against the wall and kissed me, pressing hard with his body. Another high-school turn-on. Electricity shot to my crotch. I was so ready. I felt his hard-on against my pubic bone and couldn't wait to touch it.

When we got to his room, I eyed his firm, round ass as he swiped his card key. I drooled over those butt cheeks. He held the door for me; as it closed behind us, he held my face and pushed those soft lips against mine. Our tongues chased each other as I got wetter and wetter. I wanted him to touch me, but he kept kissing. His hand went to my back and pulled me hard against him. I reached down and grabbed that hot ass. It was everything that it advertised. Firm but squeezable. I loved the way it filled up my hands.

He kiss-moaned and pulled away. He picked up my hand and led me to the bed, pushing me gently to sit at the edge of the fluffy white comforter and then lie down. His room was a little bigger than mine, with the same tan paint and identical sea-turtle painting. Silently and slowly, he unbuttoned my top button and then the next, then the next. Silk or not, I wanted to rip my sweater off for him, but I lay there, looking at those incredibly green eyes focused on my body as I let him undress me.

"You're beautiful," he said as he finished and my sweater parted.

I didn't know what to say, but I didn't have to, because he bent over me and put me in lip heaven. He pushed my sweater off my shoulders and then pulled back a second until he found my bra clip. Thankfully it was a front clasp, or I'd have died of desire by the time he took it off. His fingers brushed my pebble-hard nipples as he slid the bra over my breasts. I gasped as his touch shot fire through my whole body. He held my waist as he kissed a path down my cleavage. I was gonna faint if he didn't touch me again soon. He stood up and took off his tie.

I felt bereft. Come back!

He held his tie over me and brushed it over my nipples. I reached out for more, but he kept teasing. He dropped the tie and started at my waist, caressing his hand up my body until he held my grateful breast in his palm. His fingers found my nipple and twisted gently as his other hand got to the other lonely boob. I arched my back as he twisted the other nipple. He watched his fingers. I don't know what was making me hotter, his touch or his eyes on my bare body. He continued to cup one breast in his hand as he switched to running his palm over the tip of my nipple.

I was sure I'd soaked through my pants by now. I moaned. He bent down to kiss me. I reached for his shirt, unbuttoning the first button and then the second. I was dying to see what was under it. He let me un-button a few more buttons; then he leaned down and took my breast in his mouth, licking my nipple. His free hand pinched the other nipple. I felt the buildup deep inside and fought it.

"Oh my God, you're gonna make me come!"

"That's the plan," he said softly.

"No, I mean right now!"

"Oh, you want me to stop?" With his chin tickling my chest, his twinkling eyes framed my nipple as I looked at him.

"No, but..."

"More like this?" He moved down on my body and unbuttoned my pants.

Relieved, I caught my breath and hissed out a single word. "Yes."

He got on his knees at the foot of the bed and slid my pants off and then got up and took the waistband of my pink polka-dotted panties in his teeth. "Like this?"

"Yes!"

He hooked both sides of my panties in his pinkies and slid them down. Then he pushed apart my knees with his hands. He stopped, looking at my wide-open pussy. Practically throbbing, it ached to be touched.

"Very nice," he said.

Oh God, I couldn't take it. He took one hand off my knee, and I spread my legs more, inviting him to it. Slowly he stroked my labia with his finger. I moaned. He got back on his knees and poised his head between my legs. "Like this?" he asked as he licked the edges of my nether lips.

I jumped at his touch. "Oh." I was beyond words. He licked around my clit, short fast strokes that drove me crazy, keeping me on the edge; then he moved down and licked lower, right at the opening to my hole. I wriggled and moaned, breathing hard. He licked all the way up, around my clit some more, and then he went in for the kill. He barely licked it, but my whole body tensed, and I exploded and squirted, moaning through short breaths.

He stopped for a second. "Ooo, a squirter! I love squirters." He looked at me over my pubic bone. "Are there more?"

I caught my breath a little. "Yes." I arched up toward his face. He smiled and dove back in. His finger slid into me and tickled my G-spot as he licked around my clit. Then his soft tongue zeroed in, and I felt the tension rise in my body. He felt me tense and picked up speed, focusing on the tip of my clit. I held my breath and willed myself to come. Then I did, the explosion radiating through my body. He moved his tongue down a bit and put another finger in me. His other hand reached under me and played with my asshole. I stayed tense, and when he licked my clit again, I came again—smaller—and collapsed.

My clit couldn't take anymore. "Stop, stop," I said.

He smiled. "Done?"

"Yeah," I breathed. He pulled his fingers out and crawled up over me. I pushed my legs together, squeezing the last bit of pleasure out.

"Can I help with that?" he said.

I grabbed his hand, put it right above my lips, and squeezed it between my legs, pushing on it as hard as I could. The tingle faded, and I released his hand. I rolled on my side and reached for his dick, but it was still in his pants. One-handed, I unbuttoned and unzipped his pants and reached into his black boxer briefs. Good girth, rock-hard, and ready, I grasped him and pulled. He let out a high-pitched moan as he caught his breath. He rolled on his back, and I leaned over and flicked his nipple with my lips. He moaned again. I kept it up and then moved to the other nipple, pulling his dick and stroking his balls with my hand. I didn't want to leave his nipple, because he was enjoying it so much, but I wanted to pay him back for all those orgasms. I moved down to his dick and put my mouth around the head.

"Oh!" His body jerked. He recovered and pushed himself deeper into my mouth. I took him in and then backed off and ran my tongue around his head. He kept moaning. Reaching down between his legs with my other hand, I rubbed below his balls and ran my finger down his ass. I pushed hard on his asshole, and he jumped and gasped. I kept doing it as I sucked him, until he put his hand on my shoulder, pulling me back. I looked up.

"Stop, stop, I have to be inside you!" He handed me a condom. "Would you put this on me, please?"

I grabbed it, ripped the package, and clamped the tip between my lips; I took his dick in my hand and brought it to my mouth, rolling the condom on. I heard an "Oh!" as I rolled it out the rest of the way, and then he pushed me down next to him and got up on his knees. He climbed between my legs and steered himself into me. I felt him fill me up and reached for his ass, grabbing what I could. He was so hot, pushing above me, concentrating. I contracted around him, and his look of concentration deepened. I let go and let myself grunt with every push.

He pushed faster, and I squeezed him again and again. I knew he was getting close. He got the sex face and jerked, cried out—I thought the whole floor could hear him—and he kept jerking. He stopped moving, looked down at me, and jerked one final time. Then he rested for a moment before he pulled out slowly.

"Oh my God," he said as he climbed off, lying down beside me. "Oh my God."

I smiled. "Are you OK?"

"I'm sorry I came so fast. I couldn't hold back."

"That's a compliment," I said. "I just wanted to make you come."

"Well, you did. You certainly did."

I giggled.

"Let me go get rid of this thing." He indicated toward the used condom as he headed to the bathroom.

I heard the toilet flush and the sink running. Was this the blowoff? Should I get dressed?

He came back to the bed and lay down facing me. "I brushed my teeth," he said, leaning in for a kiss.

Interesting. When do I get my walking papers?

"That. Was. Amazing," he said, giving me a long, lazy kiss.

"Yeah," I said, "it was."

His eyes were twinkling. "Can I ask you something?"

"Yeah, sure," I replied.

"Where'd you learn to do that thing?"

"What thing?" I smiled.

"You know..."

"With my tongue? Or the other thing?"

"Both."

I giggled. "I don't kiss and tell."

He laughed, trailing kisses along my jaw. "Can I ask you something else? How many times did you come?"

It was my turn to laugh. "Three."

He smiled, his pride showing.

"Can I ask *you* something?" I said.

"Shoot."

"Why were you so interested in my work?"

"Change the subject?" he asked. "I get the hint. OK. I'd seen your name around a lot. I told you I'd read a lot of your articles. I thought you were really smart. And I'm interested in hydrogen."

"Oh."

His eyes twinkled. "But I never expected you to look like you do. Most women in our field have hairy legs and wear Birkenstocks all the time. When I saw how hot you were, I had to get to know you better."

"But I'm not your type."

"Really?" He propped up his head on his hand. "What *is* my type, Miss Pappas?"

"Well, the women I've seen you date are all gorgeous and skinny."

"OK, first of all, I don't date those women; I sleep with them. Second, there is nothing I love more than brains and curves. Especially yours." He kissed me.

"So why don't you date brainy, curvy women?"

"Again, I don't date those other women. But the reason I choose them is that there's no danger of falling for them. They're not my type— their bodies or their minds."

"I see." My mind raced. *Falling*?

"And I know that makes me sound like an asshole, but a guy's gotta get laid."

"I don't think you're an asshole. Everybody's gotta get laid."

"That's a relief." He smiled and winked. "Hey, what's your agenda for tomorrow? Are you going to the first session?"

"Yeah, I'm here to represent us at all the sessions."

He leaned over and kissed me. "Blow it off."

"What? Why?"

"Stay over. Tomorrow morning we can sleep late, maybe work up an appetite? And order room service."

Huh. Why? "But I'm supposed to be there."

"Tell them you were with me. You had a breakfast meeting. We were discussing a grant." He took my hand and kissed it.

"Are you giving us a grant?" Jesus, what were the implications of that?

"I've thought about it, but no, that's not my point. Your boss will never object to soliciting a grant."

I frowned and nodded. "That's true."

He moved closer. "Stay."

More amazing sex? "OK."

"Let me get the menu. We have to order overnight, or we might as well order lunch, because that's what time it'll come." He rolled off the bed, grabbed the hotel guide and a pen, and pulled out the room-service menu. He got back on the bed facedown, propping himself up on his elbows, pen between his fingers, with the aqua door-tag menu in front of him. "OK, what do you want? And don't just order fruit. I hate it when women think they need to diet." He looked at me, eyes sparkling. "Besides, like I said, we're gonna work up an appetite."

I giggled. "OK."

"Pancakes. How about pancakes? Everybody likes pancakes."

"OK."

He checked pancakes. "Coffee or tea?"

"Coffee."

He checked pot of coffee. "Juice?"

"No."

"OK, done." He got up and hung the menu outside the door. He wore a big smile as he jumped back in bed. "I have an extra toothbrush."

Of course he did, I thought.

"I really wanna stay up and talk, but you wore me out."

"OK."

He got up again, went into the bathroom, and came out with a brand-new toothbrush, still in the package. I took it, brushed with his whitening toothpaste, and got ready for bed. He had the lights off when I returned to bed. He reached for me and kissed me. "I wanna hold you, but I can't fall asleep like that. And like I said, you really tired me out."

Hold me? Seriously? That sounded like a line. "That's OK; neither can I." It was true.

"Oh good." He leaned in and kissed me slowly. "Good night," he whispered.

"Good night."

He rolled over, and so did I. My mind was racing. Sex always gave me a burst of energy, and his actions were not helping. He made such a distinction between sex and dating; was this a date? But he slept with me too. And what about all that afterward? That was weird. Would he have kissed me so much if it were just sex? Maybe he just likes kissing. He asked me to stay, but he was thinking sex in the morning, so that didn't help at all. But what about holding me? Did he say that to all the girls? Of course he did. I can't imagine that he'd feel obligated. What the hell? Fortunately the after-sex energy was short-lived, because I was starting to crash. I let my mind go and drifted to sleep.

2

Breakfast Meeting

When I opened my eyes, somebody was stroking circles on my back. I felt a kiss on my shoulder and the scratchy brush of facial hair.

"Good morning," Nick said, peeking over my shoulder as the night started to come back to me. Holy shit, that was real. I bagged Nick Martone. I felt the echoes of it in my body. It was good. Sooo good.

"Good morning," I said, rolling onto my back. Just woke up and he still looked hot. His hair was a little lopsided, but his eyes still twinkled, and his sleepy smile drew me to him.

"Don't I get a kiss?" he asked, leaning toward me.

I kissed him and sunk into those lips. Mmmm. He draped his hand over my body.

"What time is it?" I asked.

"Around eight thirty."

"The first session starts in half an hour."

He kissed me again, his tongue playing with mine.

I reconsidered. "The second session starts at ten thirty."

"That's more like it," he said just before our lips touched again. "Room service comes at nine, so we've got about half an hour. Then we can have breakfast and get cleaned up and ready."

That's right; there was some mention of morning sex. "Mmmm," I said, stretching and rolling over on my side. His eyes locked onto my nipples. I could feel the moisture between my legs.

He caught my leg between his, pulled me closer, and started a long kiss, playing with my tongue. Just like last night, a jolt shot to my crotch. Was I gonna make a wet spot before we even started? We kept kissing and kissing. In between kisses, he'd say things like "You're so sexy" or "You're beautiful," and I'd say something brilliant and original, like "You're so hot."

I played with his thick, wavy hair for a while; then I ran my hand down his chest to his nipple. I stroked it with my finger, pinching it a little. I wished I had a piece of ice, but just the pinching made him catch his breath. I kept flicking his nipple and rolling it between my fingers. After I'd teased him long enough, I reached down and grabbed his hard-on, grasping and pulling as he moaned. I kept playing with it but pulled away from his embrace to go down on him. He grabbed my shoulder.

"Sit on my face," he said.

I gave him a puzzled look. "Really?" I worried it would reveal the true shape of my thighs; plus that was pretty intimate. I mean, yeah, we were pretty intimate last night. But sitting on his face? We'd just met.

"A gentleman always lets the lady come first," he said. "Go ahead."

In for a dime, in for a dollar. "OK." He slid down off the pillow as I straddled his head, and he got his hands free. He looked up at me.

"Oh my God, you're so hot," he said as his eyes made their way from my face down my body and finally rested on my pussy. I thought I'd collapse from the torture of waiting.

His tongue stroked the lips at the entrance of my hole. He kept licking softly while his hands made their way up to my breasts. He kneaded them a little before focusing on my nipples. As he twisted and pinched softly, he trailed his tongue up toward my clit. He licked the sides, just like last night. Damn, this guy knew how to tease! He licked just below it.

I thought I would fall down if he didn't touch my clit soon. And then he did, and I couldn't hold back any longer. I couldn't breathe, but I exploded as the orgasm sent shivers through my body. I didn't squirt this time, thank God. I really didn't want to squirt on his face. Talk about intimate.

He kept going. I couldn't take anymore. "No, no, stop." I felt his hot breath on my box as he laughed. He moved one hand below my pubic bone and squeezed. I pushed against it as the rest of the pleasure radiated through me. I dropped onto my hands and knees, ready to climb off.

"Stay on top," he said. "I want you to ride me. Now."

"OK." Seriously? I had never seen anybody resist a blow job like he did.

As I climbed down, he reached over to the nightstand and got a condom. "Put this on, please?" He handed it to me. I unwrapped it and held the tip; as I rolled it over his rock-hard dick, he grunted and jerked. I positioned myself, held him, and guided him in.

His dick felt huge as it filled me up. I started to pump, and he helped me, grunting, moaning, and breathing hard. He looked at me like he was starving and I was a giant turkey leg. "I love watching your tits bounce," he said. He watched a little longer and then reached his hands up to knead them, still pumping hard. I squeezed him, eliciting a moan. "Do it again; I'm so close!" I clenched again, exhaling as I released. His face tensed, so I squeezed a third time. "Oh yeah, oh yeah. I'm gonna come!" He made his sex face as he jerked inside of me, again and again and again. "OK, OK, climb off, climb off."

I lay down next to him. He was still breathing heavy. "That's it," he said, still huffing. "No more sex today."

"Uh, was there more sex on the agenda?"

He smiled, his eyes dancing. "Oh yeah. Didn't you get the e-mail? I attached the agenda."

"I haven't checked my e-mail," I said.

"It's in your inbox."

I laughed and propped myself up on my elbow. "OK."

"Good, good. As long as we're on the same page." He was breathing normally. "What time is it?"

I looked at the clock. "Eight forty-four."

"Oh good. I'm starving." He reached for me. "Come over here," he said, pulling me to him. My head rested on his shoulder.

We didn't talk, but the silence was surprisingly comfortable. I couldn't stop thinking. What did he want from me? Sex, obviously, but was it my imagination or did he want more? Not according to his reputation. Maybe he's just exhibiting his player charms. Make her think she's important, right? Romance her. I was falling for it. That was all. And it stopped right here.

"Are you flying out tonight?" he said.

"Tomorrow morning."

"Do you have plans for dinner?"

What? "I thought you said no more sex today."

He looked stern. "I said *dinner*, not bed."

"Oh. No, I don't have dinner plans."

"OK then," he said. "Have dinner with me."

What the hell? Couldn't hurt, I guess. Better than eating alone. "OK."

"Good." He hugged me a little tighter.

Somebody knocked at the door. "Room service!"

Nick extracted himself, put on his underwear and shorts, and looked over at me. He grabbed his white shirt from last night and handed it to me. "Put this on," he said. I found my panties first and then threw the shirt on over my head.

He answered the door and directed the young Hispanic waiter toward the table. He turned around to look for his wallet. The waiter admired Nick's naked back, and his eyes lingered on Nick's ass. Not that I could blame him. It was a great ass, round, tight, and squeezable. When Nick turned around, the waiter's eyes gravitated toward his firm pecs and studied his abs before resting on his package. Unfazed, Nick signed the receipt and handed him a tip.

When the door was closed behind him, I said, "Did you see how he was checking you out?"

"Yeah, I practically felt it. I'm on *fire* today!"

I laughed. "Well, you *are* pretty hot."

"Takes one to know one," he said, reaching for my hand. I stood up, and he stepped back to admire me in his shirt. "Oh my God, you're so sexy!" He pulled me to him, held me tight, and kissed me. "Did I say no sex today? Because I changed my mind."

I laughed again. "Yeah, I knew that wouldn't last."

"Seriously, you look so hot in my shirt. I can't keep my hands off you."

"Do you want me to change?" I raised my eyebrows.

"No, don't change. Ever."

I giggled and kissed him. "I thought you were hungry."

"Isn't that what I was just saying?" His eyes twinkled as he looked over at the table. "OK, let's eat."

We sat down and began to spread butter and pour syrup. "Did you see Barbara Haiche yesterday?" he asked.

"Oh yeah, what was that?"

He got another pancake. "Somebody needs to tell her that Birkenstocks are not appropriate for a conference."

"Especially when you're leading a panel! Oh God, and if she's not gonna shave her legs, she should at least wear some panty hose."

We gossiped about colleagues, laughed, and talked some business. He wanted to know even more about my articles and my work. We talked about that for a while and then switched gears.

"So what does Angie Pappas do for fun?"

"Hmm, well, I hike, I sail, I cook, and I play pool. But mostly, I hang out with my club, raising money for charity."

"You cook?"

That was his takeaway? There were so many more interesting things in that sentence. "Yes, I do."

"Would you cook for me sometime back home?"

"Um, I guess so." He wants to get together at home? Future plans? Dammit, what's up with this guy? The confusion must've shown on my face.

"I'm a bachelor. I don't get many home-cooked meals."

I guess not. It wasn't like Project Runway was going to throw down some pot roast. OK then. I *did* enjoy his company. "Sure, I'll cook for you."

"It's a date." Was it? What did he mean? A real date? Or was it just an expression?

We were almost done eating when he said, "Let's take a shower."

"Um, I'm gonna have to say no."

"Why?"

"I don't have any clothes here." Duh.

"So?"

"How am I gonna get back to my room?"

"The pool's on this floor. Wear one of the robes and act like you're coming from the pool. Besides, everybody's downstairs."

Man, this guy had an answer for everything. And looking at his bare chest was wearing me down.

"OK."

"Yaaay!" He grinned and jumped up and down on his chair. My God, he was like a ten-year-old. His playful side was fun. Nice to know there was more to him than a successful overachiever. "Come on." He got up, took my hand, and led me to the white-tiled bathroom.

He turned on the water, ducked out of the bathtub, and held both of my hands apart, looking at me in his shirt. "The only thing I like better than seeing it on"—he took the top button in hand—"is taking it off."

I giggled. He continued to unbutton me, holding me at arm's length so he could admire his work. When he finished with the buttons, he slid the shirt off my shoulders, got down on one knee, and pulled off my panties. He looked up at me. "I love this view," he said.

All I could think about was that I would stay facing him so he wouldn't see my cellulite. He stood up, tested the water, switched it to shower, and ducked back out. I stood on my tiptoes and kissed him; then I slid his shorts down his legs. He was hard again. Wow. Not bad for a guy in his thirties.

"After you," he said, gesturing to the shower. Crap. I sidestepped into the tub and turned to face the shower head. He stepped in with his back to the spray. I loved watching the water bounce on his strong shoulders, his hair catching the drops like he'd been in a snowstorm. He pulled me to him and kissed me, tongue exploring my mouth, hard-on sticking into my belly. Growling, he reached down and squeezed my ass before reaching for the soap.

He sudsed up his hands and ran them over my back and butt, pulling me even closer to him. I took the opportunity to knead his ass. Man, was it sexy! He picked up the soap and soaped up again. This time he ran his hands over my collarbone, down to my breasts. He made little circles on my nipples with his palms; then he took the weight of my full breasts in his hands and kissed me. He let my breasts go gently and slid his hands down my torso, my belly, and down to my lips. He stroked them, and my whole pussy ached for more action. He slid his finger over my clit, and I jumped. Then his hand left my body, and he reached for the soap and handed it to me. "Your turn."

I stepped up to him and rubbed my body on his; I kissed him and stepped back. I sudsed and ran my fingers over his firm pecs. He had the perfect amount of chest hair—enough for a shadow but not enough for a rug. I flattened my hands and ran them over his nipples. I got some more soap and slid my hands from his pecs and over the bumps of his six-pack, exploring it for the first time. Slowly I slid my hands down along either side of his happy trail, meeting in the middle just above his prick. His knees buckled a little as I took it in both hands. He moaned as I stroked it, and I moved one hand over his balls. I loved watching him lean his head back and moan as I played some more; then I let go and picked up the soap again.

I got soap on my hands and started at his shoulders, moving down through the cuts in his hardened arms and back up, over his shoulders and down his back. When I got to the small of his back, I pulled him to me and kissed him, feeling his dick poke my belly. I let go, got some more soap, and ran my hands over his ass, feeling every curve of it, and then I pulled him back to me.

"What do you wanna do?" I asked.

"I wanna fuck you."

"I thought you said no more sex."

"I said I changed my mind."

I cupped my hands, filled them with water, and rinsed his dick. "Come on," I said.

My whole pussy was still on high alert.

"Hang on," he said, sweeping the shower curtain open and stepping one foot out on the bath mat.

I only saw his lower half as his torso twisted and stretched out toward the counter. He ducked back in, holding up a condom, already unwrapped. *Oh, right, almost forgot that one.*

"Good call," I said as he slid the condom on.

He reached out and pulled me to him, hard. He shoved himself into me, and I wrapped around him, feeling the friction. He pumped and pumped, and my nipples reached toward him as my lower lips swelled around him. His face seized up, and he pulled out, drooping. "I don't have anything left." He planted a hand on the wall to hold himself up. "No more sex today. I mean it this time."

"Can I get some water?" I asked. He turned sideways to let me by. I steadied myself on the wall as my overworked calves almost gave out, and I rinsed myself off. "Do you need to wash your hair?"

"Shit, no, I can hardly stand up. You wore me out."

"OK." I didn't need to wash my hair either. My hairdresser said to wash curls every other day. "Want me to turn this off?"

He stood up and smiled. "No, I have to shave."

"OK, I'll get out." I grabbed the shower curtain.

"No. Don't." He stood up, and we switched places. He squirted some shaving cream into his hand and soaped up. I enjoyed the view and cupped his ass. "I said no sex!" he teased.

"I'm just playing." I watched as he shaved his face and neck, working around his goatee; then he rinsed. He turned off the water and turned around.

"Now you can get out." He swept the curtain aside.

I did as I was told. He climbed out after me and grabbed a towel. He opened it up, put it around me, and gave me a long hug from behind. He put his chin over my shoulder, and I turned and kissed him. "Wow," he said. "Just wow. You're amazing."

I giggled. "You called the play; I just ran it."

"Ooo, football metaphor. You just get better and better."

He grabbed another towel. I admired his body as he toweled off. I loved the way his muscles moved under his skin. I walked out of the bathroom. I didn't want to put on my dirty underwear, but I also didn't want to walk back to my room, in just a robe, without it. I put it on inside out and got the white terry robe off the hook on the bathroom door.

"Can I help you with that?" he asked, still naked.

"Sure." I handed the robe to him, and he held it as I put it on. I closed it up. "OK, I gotta go. Shit, I can't pull off the pool story carrying my clothes."

He went to the closet for a laundry bag, gathered my clothes, and put them in it. "These are your pool accoutrements."

I was impressed. "Good thinking."

"I guess this is it," he said. "I'll see you downstairs?"

"Yeah, see you downstairs."

"And tonight?"

Oh my God, why did I agree to that? It was probably a way to let me down easy. And dammit, I couldn't think of an excuse fast enough to say no. "And tonight."

He came closer. In a low voice, he said, "OK, see you later," and kissed me.

"Yeah," I said. "See you later."

I left and headed toward my room. Luckily, I didn't see anyone I knew in the hall or the elevator. Despite my reservations, I couldn't get over the feeling that Nick wanted more than my body. As I dressed, I turned it over and over in my mind. Why did he want to have dinner? Dinner could lead to sex. And why did he want me to stay for breakfast last night? Breakfast is polite after sex, but he was so little-kid excited after I said I'd stay. That could have been an excuse for morning sex, though. Not that any woman wants to pig out with someone who's just seen her naked.

There was something about the way he held me, too—like he couldn't get me close enough. And all that silence. And what was with the future plans? Cook for him? Really? That could lead to sex too, and probably would, but you don't seduce a woman by making her the workhorse. Not that he had to seduce me. That was quite possibly the best sex I'd ever had.

When I was done with my makeup, I got dressed and went downstairs. I was late for the session, so I tiptoed into the back row. The speaker was boring, and my mind wandered to the sex, reliving it over and over. He'd said he had an early flight tomorrow, but I hoped sex wasn't really off the table for tonight. Unless dinner was just a way to let me down easy. But a guy like him would go for the last lay, wouldn't he?

We had a keynote speaker at lunch, and Nick caught my eye from across the room and winked. I winked back. He turned back to his lunch companion, talking business apparently, with their heads together and brows furrowed. I ate my rubber chicken and exchanged business cards and pleasantries with my table mates, all the while thinking about what I'd wear to dinner.

There was a break after lunch, and I went outside with some colleagues. Almost everybody was out there. It was a nice day, and we craved sunshine; plus the hotel was so over-air-conditioned that we were all freezing. I was talking to Sharon Burke, a sustainable transportation lobbyist. I liked Sharon a lot, but man, could she talk! I felt a hand on my shoulder. I looked back and buckled a little when I saw it was Nick. He asked Sharon, "Can I steal her for a second?"

"Sure, sure," she said.

"I'll see you later," I told her, as Nick waited for me.

Oh God, was dinner cancelled? Of course. This was it. The blowoff. In spite of myself, I did feel let down.

"Walk with me," he said, leading me inside. We went past the conference room to the pay-phone banks, which, for some reason, the hotels still maintained when most everybody had cell phones. We were completely alone. "I know you want to be discreet. I made the dinner reservation. Can I pick you up at six thirty?"

I was surprised at how relieved I felt. "Yeah, six thirty's fine."

"OK, see you then." He glanced around, grabbed my arms, pushed me against the wall and kissed me, his tongue insistent. God, I loved the way he kissed. "Sorry. I couldn't wait," he said, his face still close to mine.

"It's OK," I said, still in a bit of shock.

He hugged me and slid his hands down my arms and squeezed. "See you later." He sauntered away.

God, this was maddening!

3

Courting a Client

The rest of the sessions were better, and they took my mind off Nick Martone. Toward the end of the last session, though, my mind wandered to my wardrobe. I didn't bring date clothes to conferences. When the sessions were over and I headed to my room, I knew what I'd wear. He liked his shirt on me so much, and I'd give him what he wanted—sort of. I got the tailored red blouse from yesterday's suit out of my suitcase and paired it with my stretchy charcoal work pants. I redid my makeup and put on some red lipstick and perfume, and I was ready. Twenty minutes early. Damn.

I thought about my date's preferred outcome, and I realized that I wouldn't have time to pack for tomorrow's flight if we wound up in bed. I got my stuff together, and then I was really ready. Ten more minutes. I flipped through the TV channels and watched a rerun of *The Golden Girls*. I was laughing when I heard a knock.

Nick wore a black suit, a green shirt that matched his eyes, and a tie that had little frogs on it. "You look fantastic," he said. "For you." He handed me a tiny box of chocolate.

"Thank you. You didn't have to do that."

"It's our first date. I wanted to bring you flowers, but you're in a hotel. What would you do with them? I'm sure your maid would have liked them, but she's not my date, so this seemed more appropriate."

I laughed. "Thank you. This is very thoughtful." I stood on my toes to kiss him. "You look fantastic too." Like a freakin' movie star I'm imagining naked.

"Are you ready?"

"Let me get my purse." I picked it up, and he held out his hand. I hesitated but then took it. What could it hurt? Pretty much everyone from the conference had left already.

We made out in the elevator, pausing at every stop. My room was on the twentieth floor. I had those lips to myself until the third, when an older couple got on with us.

We went to a steak-and-seafood restaurant, done in men's club brass and dark wood, with white tablecloths and candles. Nick asked me to pick the wine. All my wine tasting in Virginia paid off. I picked a Viognier, and the waiter was quick with the bottle.

"Cheers," Nick said, holding his glass.

"Cheers." We clinked and then studied our menus.

"What are you gonna get?" he asked.

"I'm thinking the halibut or the lamb chops."

He skimmed the menu. "Lamb looks good, but I'd go with the halibut. It's so much fresher on the West Coast."

"Mmmm," I said, "good point. Halibut it is."

"That's right; you're Greek, aren't you?"

I whipped my head up from the menu, startled by the complete non sequitur. "What?"

Nick smiled. "Lamb. Most Americans don't like lamb, but Greeks love lamb."

"Very perceptive," I said. "Yes, I'm Greek, and yes, we eat lamb a lot."

"I know. I'm half Greek."

I blinked. "You are?"

"Come on, my name is Nick."

Really? Lots of people are named Nick. "Yeah, but Martone is Italian."

"There are plenty of Italian Nicks," he said. "What part of Greece is your family from?"

Typical Greek question. "You *are* Greek. Ithaca. What about you?"

The waiter came, poured our wine, and took our order. I went with the halibut.

"My mother's Greek; my dad's Italian. Corfu."

I'd been to Corfu. It was beautiful, and right across the Ionian Sea from Ithaca. "We're neighbors."

"How many Angies in your family?"

That scene in *My Big Fat Greek Wedding* where everybody had the same names was absolutely dead-on. "Six. How many Nicks?"

"Four. Diner?"

I took a sip of wine. I'd chosen well. "My grandfather had several. You?"

"None."

"That's too bad." I winked. "So did your mom pin a Greek eye to your underwear when you were a kid?"

His laughter was infectious. "Those pins always came apart and stabbed me. But you never know when you'll have to fend off the evil eye."

How Greek was he really? "Always when you least expect it. Do you speak Greek?"

"A little. More when I was a kid, and I heard it from my mom's family. You?"

"Same thing. I understand a lot now, but I have to be around it to really speak. Did they spit on you whenever you got a compliment?"

"Of course they did. In fact, I almost did it to you when you answered the door. You were—are—so beautiful."

"Thanks for your restraint." I smiled. God, he was easy to talk to.

The busboy came by and dropped off our bread. "Greek and Italian. So it must have been a regular food fest at your house. Did your mom cook mostly Greek?"

"It was...is a food fest. My mom is a fantastic cook. She cooks Greek and Italian, but my dad always makes the gravy. He doesn't want her to mess with it. Sunday tradition, you know. My mom would like you. You two could talk about cooking for hours, I'd imagine."

I snorted, and the wine went up my nose. His *mother*? Would like me? Where did *that* come from?

I recovered. "Gravy. Wow, haven't heard marinara called that outside of New York."

"New Jersey," he corrected.

I took a piece of bread. Grilled and crunchy. Nice. "Right. Where in Jersey?"

"Bergen County. North Jersey."

"I know where that is. So what did your parents do for a living there?"

"My dad was a mechanic. He was a partner in a service station. He's retired now. My mom stayed at home."

So his family didn't fund the trust. Interesting. How much would he give up? "Oh, so how'd you go to Cornell?" Oops. It was common knowledge, but I should've let him tell me.

He stopped tearing his bread and raised his eyebrows. "How'd you know I went to Cornell?"

"Come on, Nick; everybody knows that."

He nodded slowly. "True. Small circles. Scholarship. I had a full scholarship to Cornell."

The busboy came by and refilled our water glasses.

"How'd you end up running the Green Trust?"

"Well, after college, I worked for Greenpeace for a while, and then my uncle asked me to start the Green Trust. He put up the money, I invested it, started to distribute it, and here I am."

So it *was* family money. "So why doesn't anybody know that?" Way to play close to the vest, Angie.

Fortunately my slip didn't faze him. "Why do I keep it quiet, you mean? I like to keep people guessing. It keeps my beneficiaries at a distance, and that ensures a fairer, more professional process in such small circles."

He certainly did keep people guessing anyway. Dammit.

He leaned in so he could lower his voice. "Seriously, and don't let this leave this table, my uncle got the money because he got mixed up with the wrong people. And before you make the assumption, he's my mother's brother, so he's not Italian. He felt so bad about how he got the money, he wanted to do some good with it." He sat back. "What about you? Where did you grow up?"

The waiter came by and poured more wine. "In the suburbs of New York City. Everyone in my town was either Irish or Italian-Sicilian."

He nodded. "That's how you know what gravy is. What did your parents do?"

"My dad designed early computer chips. My mom directed the choir for the church."

He leaned forward again in interest. "And where did you go to school?"

"NYU."

"Ah, a city girl. What's your degree in?"

"Journalism. After school I wrote obituaries for the *Poughkeepsie Journal*; then I got a reporting job and moved to DC."

He nodded slowly. "Reporter. That explains all the questions."

I smiled and blushed. "I'm not the only one asking questions."

He started again. "Fair enough, how'd you wind up at Hydrogen Futures?"

"My boss recruited me. He liked my work in the trade journals. He used to be one of my sources. He needed someone who could research and write."

"And here you are."

"And here I am."

He held up his glass. "To being here. With me."

"Cheers."

Our food arrived, looking scrumptious. Nick went on with the questions. "So, did your mom cook Greek food?"

I laughed. "Sort of. She made some Greek dishes, but she was a terrible cook. We'd eat spaghetti and mashed potatoes with ketchup, and she'd broil all of our meat without any seasoning."

"*Sketoh*? Oh, the horror! Is that why you learned to cook?"

I shrugged. "You know, I never thought about it that way. That was probably a factor, but it was more that I liked to eat." Great, Angie, draw attention to your appetite and your weight.

"Doesn't everybody like to eat?" Perfect answer. I felt a little less like a fat chick.

"Oh God, my mom didn't. She only ate weird stuff, like parsley salad and sour cream with sugar. And if you took her to a restaurant, she'd read the menu for an hour and then order two eggs over easy."

He nodded. "So you cooked out of survival."

"And interest. I love food." Again, Tubby? Nice.

"Me too. And I like that in a woman." Another perfect answer. Man, he was a charmer.

He pointed his fork at my plate. "How's your halibut?"

"Really good. How's your steak?"

"Fantastic. Do you want a bite?"

Oh, so we're at this point already? Well, OK. "Sure; do you want some halibut?"

"Yeah, bring it." He speared a bite of steak and held out his fork. I made a motion to bring it to my plate, but he shook his head. "Uh-uh. Open."

It took me a minute to realize he was talking about my mouth. I opened.

His eyes sparkled as he fed me the steak. The rub on it was amazing. It was a perfect medium-rare; it was tender, and it had just the right amount of fat. The gesture was sweet and intimate, and it made me feel more like a date, less like a conquest.

"Isn't it good?" he said.

I nodded. I was still chewing.

"Sorry."

"It's OK," I said after I finished. "That was amazing. I wish I'd ordered it."

He pointed his fork at my plate. "You said yours was good."

"It is but not as good as that." I had entree envy.

"Lemme try."

I got him a bite, and he leaned closer, mouth open. I fed him. God, what a flirt!

"That's really good," he said when he finished chewing. "Really fresh."

"It's a great sauce too." It was. Asian-inspired, sweet, and salty. It complemented the fish perfectly.

We talked some more about food, growing up, our environmental goals, and hobbies. We flirted and laughed, and conversation came easy. This was a real date. I followed his lead and resisted sexual innuendo, but the more I looked at him, the more I wanted him. We were too full for dessert; so after Nick paid, we just got a cab back to the hotel. I kissed him in the cab and expected to make out, but we mostly held hands. We did kiss in the elevator. When we got to my door, he took my face in his hands and pushed those sweet lips against mine and gave me a proper tongue lashing.

He looked concerned. "You have an early flight, right?"

"It's not *that* early. What about you?" Say no. Say no!

"I have a morning meeting, and I'm flying out at one."

My turn to make a move. "Would you like to come in?" Please! What was with him?

His shoulders relaxed as he exhaled. "Oh thank God! Yes, I'd like to come in."

I swiped my card key, and he held the door. My room was almost identical to Nick's. The door opened to a small hallway, vanity, and bathroom to the right. My full bed, smaller than Nick's queen, sat facing the huge entertainment center that held the TV, a tight squeeze between them to reach the desk and chair by the window. The decor wouldn't win any prizes; it was a basic hotel room, with fluffy white comforter, gold blackout curtains, and obligatory flower painting over the bed.

Nick put his arms around me as the door closed behind us and kissed me, our tongues teasing. I took his hand and led him to the foot of the bed, pushed him to sitting, and moved in to undress him. His face was in my cleavage.

"Oh, I like this!" he said, unbuttoning my shirt and pushing his face in between my boobs.

"You're gonna like this even better," I said, taking off his jacket and tie and unbuttoning his shirt. It was my turn to look at his body. I pushed him down to his back.

"I feel like I'm gonna get tied up." His voice was teasing.

I raised my eyebrows. "That can be arranged."

"Ooo, I like the sound of that."

I reached for his tie. "OK, well, there are no bedposts, but I guess I could just do this." I tied his hands together over his head. "Now you're mine."

He gave me an innocent look. "I wasn't before that?"

"Shut up."

"Ooo, dominating. I like that."

I unbuckled his pants, unbuttoned, unzipped, and pulled them off, revealing tight red boxer briefs. My favorite, but those had to come off too. I petted his hard-on through them before I pulled them off. "Move up on the bed. I don't do knees."

"Yes, mistress." He scooted up. I climbed up next to him and grabbed his dick. I jerked him with that hand and stroked his balls with the other. "Oh," he moaned.

I leaned down and licked the head of his penis. Another moan. I licked around the edge. He moaned and writhed. I took the whole head in my mouth, while I continued to pump and stroke his balls. He moaned and writhed more forcefully, lifting his hips toward my mouth. I ran my hand down to his ass, fondling the outside of the hole before poking my finger in. He jumped. "Oh God!" It wasn't even a minute later when he cried, "Stop! Stop!"

I looked up. "Why?"

"I'm gonna come."

I tilted my head and eyed him sardonically. "That is the point, Nick."

"No, I-you first. Come on!"

Uh..."OK."

"Untie me. I'm dying to touch you."

I straddled and untied him, taking special care to sit right on his dick. As soon as the tie was loose, he pulled me down to him, kissed me, and said, "Oh my God, you've gotta stop. I'm gonna come all over you."

I raised my eyebrows. "Is that a problem?"

"I said I wanted to do you, woman! Now get off me so I can properly finger you."

"Oh, look who's dominating now!" I slid off and lay down next to him. He rolled over to face me, and I helped him take off my pants and panties. He reached down to my hole, stroking the outside of my lips on the way. I inhaled as his finger went in me. He moved it in and out, stuck another finger in, and reached for my G-spot. I moaned when he found it, and I started to feel the buildup inside.

He leaned in, kissed me, and sucked my tongue. That, coupled with the G-spot, was almost too much, but then he bent down, popped my breast out of my bra, and caught my nipple between his lips. I grunted and moaned as he squeezed and licked it. I came, and the energy radiated out from my G-spot. He pulled his fingers out and stroked up to my clit. He continued to caress it as he came back up to kiss me.

"Didja like that?"

"Yes," I breathed.

"Are there more?"

"Yes." He kept caressing with one hand and reached the other to the neglected nipple. I arched my back as he brushed the top of it. He started to roll it between fingers. I felt the orgasm deep in my clit. He kept rubbing and rolling and leaned down to lick my other nipple. The energy rose to the surface. I writhed around as he kept stroking, and it hit me. I couldn't breathe, as it rocked my whole body. "Stop, stop; I'm done."

He put his hands between my legs. "Any of this?"

"I don't think so. I think that was all."

"Are you ready to be fucked?"

I took a deep breath. "Oh yeah."

He climbed off the bed and found his pants, took out a condom, climbed back on, and straddled me. I watched him put the condom on, and he was still stiff as a flagpole. I'd expected him to have lost some of his erection after the BJ-interruptus. I loved looking at him. He was a chiseled masterpiece.

He nudged my legs apart and got in between. He guided himself in, and he really felt like a flagpole. He started pumping and put my legs up on his chest. "I love the way you look down there," he said, hugging and kissing my legs. "I can see everything."

I squeezed him, and he grunted and almost lost his balance. "I love that too!" he said with a chuckle.

I reached up and played with his nipples. His face concentrated a little more, and he moved my legs back down to the bed, shifting to missionary and speeding up. I reached up to his arms, feeling the strength in his hard muscles as he held himself up. I squeezed some more, grunting with every push. I didn't see it coming. "Aaaugh!" He jerked a few times and stopped. "That is *it*! No more sex today!"

I laughed. He was still inside.

"Stop that!" he said. "I can't take anymore."

I gave him a playful smile. "Sorry."

He pulled out. "I guess I can forgive you."

I nodded solemnly. "Thank you. You're a real generous guy."

This time, he laughed. When he caught his breath, he rolled on his side to face me. "You're amazing," he said.

"So are you."

He propped himself up on one elbow. "So when am I coming over for dinner?"

"I don't know. Did you wanna set something up right now?" That would be ridiculous.

"Yeah, I know you've got an early flight, and I don't want to forget when you kick me out."

"Lemme get my Blackberry." He got up to get his too. I checked my calendar. "I'm free on the twenty-fourth."

His face fell. "Really? Nothing sooner?"

Really? "Um, next Saturday."

"That's perfect. I'll bring the wine. E-mail me your address and phone number when you get back to the office."

How was he this pushy right after sex? In a softer voice, he asked, "Do you mind if I stay a little longer?"

"No, I want you to stay." Oops.

He jumped back on the bed. "Good." He reached out his arm and pulled me to him. "Come closer." He kissed me.

After the kiss ended, I said, "Can I ask you something?"

He squeezed my arm. "Anything."

"Why do you resist blow jobs?"

He laughed. "I didn't resist this one."

"No, but before. You stopped me. Twice."

"Oh. Well, making you come makes me so hot that by the time you're done, I'm way past that point. I wanna be in you, with you; I wanna look at you."

Huh. "Oh."

His turn. "Can I ask you a question?"

"Yeah, sure." I said.

"Why are you holding back?"

"What? I'm not holding back."

"Yes, you are," he said.

Where was he going with this? "I just had sex with you four times in two days. How is that holding back?"

"No, you're right. You're definitely not holding back sex. But I'm not talking about sex. I'm talking about you. And me."

"What about you and me?" I was getting that nagging feeling again.

"You're holding back on you. I want to know more about you, and you're not giving it up."

"Yes, I am," I said, a little too forcefully.

"I don't want to argue, but I'd like to hear more, OK?"

"OK."

God, did he really like me?

He rubbed my back. "I don't want to, but I guess I should let you sleep, so you don't miss your flight tomorrow." He let me go and got up to get dressed. "Hey, are you going to that meeting over at Wind Power on Wednesday?"

That was my job. "Yeah, I was planning on it. Why, are you?"

He smiled. "Yeah, I'm working with them right now, so I've got to attend the meetings." He raised his eyebrows. "Can I sit next to you and play footsie under the table?"

I winked at him. "I'd be mad if you didn't." I threw on my pajama top so I could walk him out. We stopped at the door.

"OK, so I'll see you Wednesday?" he asked.

Yep. "See you Wednesday."

"And then next Saturday?" Man, he had a serious need for some home cooking.

"Yes, next Saturday."

"OK, safe flight." He gave me a long, lingering kiss.

"Good night."

I couldn't wait for Wednesday.

4

Intimate Meeting

$\mathcal{I}$ got off the Metro at Farragut West and headed to the office. Yesterday was maybe the longest day of my life. But now it was Wednesday, and only a few hours kept me from seeing Nick at the Alliance meeting. I'd worn a white button-down shirt and a green plaid skirt. I rarely wore skirts to work, but I wanted to look nice for Nick. As I cut through the park where the bike messengers hung out smoking pot, one of them said, "Hel-lo!"

Well, operation wardrobe: successful.

We had our morning staff meeting, and I did some research, but I kept getting distracted. I maintained an e-mail conversation with my friend Julia, but I didn't tell her about Nick. She was in the environmental community too, and I didn't want to tell anyone. If people knew, I'd look like a fool, because everybody knew Nick was a player. Plus, if we ever got a grant from his foundation, everyone would think I earned it on my back.

Mmmm, on my back with Nick.

I left early for the meeting. Tourists thought the Metro was super-convenient, but at midday, you could wait half an hour for a train. I read my book while I waited. For once I was happy that the train took forever. I didn't want to be late, but I didn't want to arrive too early either and have to wander around like an idiot.

In the end, I only got to the meeting a few minutes early, so I put my stuff down and got some water. The table was still pretty empty, and no one was paying attention, so I sat in the chair next to my stuff, saving a place for Nick. I chatted with my friend Melissa. She was a lobbyist for hydrogen, too, so we met often for expense-account lunches. Her lobbying was sponsored by one company, determined to gain market share, so she got the big expense account. She could take me out because I worked for the industry as a whole, so we ostensibly discussed industry trends and competing technology, but we rarely did. We rarely saw each other outside of work, so those lunches were our social life together.

"How was the conference?" Melissa asked. She always looked cute, with her bright blue eyes, wavy brown bob, and spray of Irish freckles. She had a few extra pounds on her too, and we'd done a few diets together. For two months, every lunch we had together was sushi. That was after Melissa learned to eat sushi. The first time she ate it, we were at a meeting and she tried to cut it with a fork. We lost some weight on those diets, but it always came back.

"Good. Most of it. We missed you."

She sighed. "Yeah, I had to go to Toronto for a company meeting."

"Too bad. Bob took us out for a nice dinner."

"I always miss the fun stuff!" she said.

"Is someone sitting here?" Nick asked me, pointing to my stuff. Damn, I didn't even see him come in, but I could smell his cologne, and I wanted him already.

"No, no, go 'head," I said, feeling the anticipation. Jesus Christ, I had to control myself! This was a business meeting.

"How are you?" he asked, all businesslike, green eyes twinkling. He was loving this game.

I could play too. "I'm good, I'm good. How was your flight?"

"Delayed. Twice."

"Oh, that sucks."

"Yeah, I didn't get back until three in the morning."

Ah, what I could do with him at three in the morning! "Oh, that's rough."

Someone across the table greeted Nick. He stood up and shook hands as they chatted a bit. I was relieved to stop thinking of neutral things to say, and happy to have such a great view of his butt. He looked fantastic, as usual, in black suit pants, a black shirt, and a royal-blue-and-black pinstriped tie.

Wind-Power Jennifer started the meeting. There were three Jennifers: Wind-Power Jennifer, Solar Jennifer, and Hydro Jen (she represented waterpower)—the nickname was an energy joke.

I opened up my notebook. Nick opened his folio and started to write. No one had said anything worth writing down. Maybe it was something from his premeeting convo. I turned my attention to Jennifer.

Nick tap-tapped his pen on the table next to me. I turned to look, and he pointed the pen at the paper.

You look beautiful!

I scribbled in my notebook as he watched.

Thank you. You look really hot!

He reached under the table and put his hand on my knee. My stomach quivered. After a few minutes, he slid his hand between my legs, reaching up my skirt and stroking my thigh. My lower half tingled, and my mind drifted back to the last time we had sex. A skirt? What was I thinking? I thought I'd leave a wet spot on the chair. I wanted to throw him down on the table and fuck him right there, but I couldn't—damn meeting. Instead, I wrote a new note.

Stop it!

He gave me an innocent look.

Stop what?

Oh, the man was aggravating.

Very funny.

He just lifted one eyebrow.

Why?

I fixed him with a glare.

Really?

He gave me a sad puppy face as he slipped his hand from between my legs and rested it back on my knee. I tried to focus on the meeting, but shots of electricity radiated from the warmth of his hand, awakening desire in my whole body. I took some actual meeting-related notes, but I also noticed my nipples were so hard that they were showing through the pads in my bra. Nick dropped his pen on the floor and slid his hand off me to climb down after it. I jumped as I felt a bite right above my knee. He was such a little kid. He hit his head on the table getting back up. I stifled a snort.

"Are you OK?" I asked neutrally as he emerged.

"Yeah, I'm fine."

He sat back down in his chair, and I couldn't resist writing one more note:

Serves you right.

He put his hand back on my lap, over the skirt but higher on the thigh. I couldn't take much more, but dammit, our date wasn't until Saturday.

"So, you got that Angie?" Jennifer asked me.

"Yeah, sure," I said. Dammit, what did she tell me to do?

The meeting ended, and people got up to leave. Nick leaned in, looking like he was talking business. "Go to the ladies' room until everyone's gone; then meet me in the elevator."

Oh thank God, I could at least get some tongue today. And we were on the tenth floor. Awesome! I gathered my stuff and went to the bathroom. As I walked in, Melissa came out of a stall, mischief in her eyes.

"So, what was going on in there?" she asked.

"Whaddaya mean?"

"Between you and Nick."

Shit. "Me and Nick?"

"Oh please, Angie. I saw it. Spill it. What's up with you two?"

I inhaled. "We hooked up at the fuels conference."

Her eyes widened. "Ooo! And you're still hooking up?"

I said softly, "I think we might be dating. But please keep it to yourself."

"Dating? Nick Martone?"

"His idea. I thought it was just a hookup, but he's acting like he wants more than that."

"Ooo, juicy!" She tented her fingers.

"Do *not* tell anyone!"

"Man, if I'd bagged Nick Martone, I'd be telling everyone." Melissa was getting married, but she was still having trouble adjusting to the idea of permanent monogamy.

"Yeah, but people talk, and it could go so many different ways. I don't want people talking about us." I shouldn't have told her.

"OK, OK. But you have to give me details. Over lunch."

"Deal. I'll send you a meeting invite when I get back to my office."

"OK, see you later." I still heard voices in the reception area, so I went to pee. My panties were soaked, as were my tights. Fortunately, my skirt was not. I heard the voices fade and the elevator door close as I washed my hands. I put on some lipstick and headed out. Nick was coming toward me from the men's room. I pushed the button, and we waited for the elevator in silence.

We stepped into the elevator. As soon as the door closed, Nick took my notebook and dropped it on the floor. Then he took my head in his hands and kissed me, hard. He pulled back and said, "You look so hot. I wanted to eat you out right there."

I grabbed his ass and pulled him closer. He pushed his hard-on against me. "Oh my God, Nick, I wanted to fuck you right on that table!"

He kissed me and fondled my breasts. My whole body tingled and ached for more. The elevator stopped, and we separated. No one was waiting. The doors closed again. He gripped low on my ass, pulling my legs apart and grabbing at my pussy. "I can't wait until Saturday. I want you right now."

I moaned a little as he kissed my neck. "Nick, I wanna fuck your brains out too, but I have to go back to work."

He kept kissing my neck, heading toward my cleavage. "Tell them you went to the gym. We'll get a hotel room."

I squeezed his ass and pulled him toward me as hard as I could. "Can't. My gym bag's in the office."

He pushed his knee between my legs. My skirt hitched up as I rode him. "They're not gonna notice that."

"It's orange, and it's right at the door. They will. Believe me, they will." My clit felt so good as I rode his knee. I ground against him as the pleasure built up. He squeezed my breast, and I shook as the energy radiated out through my body.

He stopped. "Did I just make you come?"

I exhaled. "Yeah. Yeah, you did." My body relaxed.

"And I'm still blue-balled?" And breathless. "Tonight. How about tonight? At my place."

"Yeah, I can do that."

He grabbed my ass and ground against me. "OK, I'll e-mail you the address. Rosslyn Metro." The elevator stopped, preparing to open. "Dammit!"

"It's OK, Nick. I'll see you tonight." I kissed those pouty lips and pulled my skirt back down. The door opened. Nick picked my notebook up and handed it to me, and we walked out into the sunshine.

"Which way you going?" he asked.

"Metro."

"I'll walk you there. It's on the way to my office." He grabbed my hand.

I looked at him, eyebrows raised. "Isn't that a little indiscreet?"

"It is, but everybody's gone."

"I guess." I squeezed his hand, and we walked.

"I'll get some takeout tonight, OK?"

He was already thinking food? "Sure, that's good."

"Whaddaya like? Italian, Chinese, Thai?"

"Why don't we just order while I'm there?"

"Oh yeah, of course." We got to the sign at the Metro entrance. He reached down around the small of my back and pulled me toward him, kissed me, and played with my tongue way too much for the street. He broke our kiss and, still holding my waist, said, "See you later."

"See you later."

"I'll e-mail you." He gave me a final quick kiss and released me.

"OK."

He'd already e-mailed his address when I got back to my office.

I got another e-mail: *As soon as you can get there, hottie ;-)*

I e-mailed back: *Probably about 5:30. Can't wait.*

I couldn't stop thinking about seeing Nick. If I left work at five, I could take the Orange Line straight over there. I was on the phone with an editor when I realized that Nick would want me to stay. I had to prepare for that, at least based on past experience. I didn't have any clothes with me, except my gym bag. My office was business-casual, not kickbox-casual. If I went home first, I'd get there at least an hour later than I'd said. I didn't want to disappoint Nick. I knew how eager he was. I'd just felt it on my leg.

I took a break to go out and buy some clothes. I wanted to breeze in and breeze out, maybe just get a new shirt and panties, but then I thought about it. If I wore my skirt tomorrow, everyone would speculate. They wouldn't know about Nick, of course, but it wasn't like I wanted everybody to know I didn't sleep at home, either.

I tried on a few pairs of pants at the Lerner down the street. I was kidding myself. They never had enough sixteens. I went next door to Lane Bryant and luckily hit with the fourth pair. Usually finding pants that flatter my Greek butt takes me hours. I picked up some panties and a shirt and headed back to the office. I worked on writing an article to take my mind off Nick.

The clock ticked slowly, but I made it to five o'clock—well, 4:45 p.m. I figured no one would mind if I left a little early. I rode the Metro to Rosslyn and walked up the gigantic escalator. Maybe the exercise would tighten up my butt and thighs. I found the building—a fairly new skyscraper. I checked out the lobby while I waited for Nick to buzz me in. Very fancy. I rode the elevator to the twenty-third floor and found his apartment. I knocked.

"Hey, come on in," he said as he held the door for me. "Whatcha got?" He pointed at my shopping bag.

"Did some shopping."

"Oh. Hi," he said and kissed me softly. I'd kind of expected him to jump me as soon as I got there, but I guessed he'd calmed down, because he walked away. I looked around. His apartment blew me away—huge living room with the prerequisite bachelor big-screen TV, black leather couches, and hardwood floors with a big black-and-white fluffy throw rug in front of the couch. One wall was all glass and led to a big balcony.

"Your apartment is amazing!" I said.

"Oh yeah, let me show you around." He was back by my side. "Champagne?"

"Ooo, thank you!" I took the glass. He held the small of my back and steered me. "This is the living room." He turned around. "And this is the kitchen." His kitchen was big for an apartment—much bigger than mine, with black granite counters—and open to the living room. He led me into the hallway. "This is the bathroom." His bathroom tile was dove-gray subway-style with river-stone accents. He had a big jetted tub, a slate counter with glass-bowl sink, and plenty of room to move. My bathroom was so small that I couldn't even undress in it. He led me to a bedroom. "This is the office slash guest room." It was robin's-egg blue with dark gray blinds and matching carpet. He had a desk, computer, office chair, and low bed in it. A Zen fountain gurgled in one corner. We took a few more steps. "And this is the master. There's another bathroom in there." I half-expected to see silk sheets, mirrored ceilings, and leopard print all over the bedroom, but it was very tastefully decorated. The walls were a very light gray. The cushy carpet was a shade darker. His four-poster bed, backed to the longest wall, facing the door, was distressed gray wood that reminded me of New England beach-house shingles, and the comforter on the perfectly made bed was a deep royal blue. His sleek silver watch sat atop the dark-wood nightstand on the left side of the bed. He had no other furniture, so there was a lot of empty space. The closet on the left wall was a typical shutter design that must've come with the apartment.

"Very nice," I said.

"Oh, let me show you the best part," he said, guiding me away from the bedroom. First time he'd ever done that. He led me back into the living room; we crossed it, and he opened the door to the balcony. We stepped outside.

"Oh my God, this is amazing, Nick!" He had an expansive view of the back of the Lincoln Memorial and the Washington Monument, Arlington Cemetery, and the Potomac, including a bird's-eye view of Roosevelt Island.

He slid his hand to my waist and pulled me closer, next to him. "Yeah, that's why I bought it. On the Fourth of July, you can sit out here and see the whole fireworks show. You should come over." The Fourth of July was like a month away. Future plans. We stood there awhile, until he moved behind me and slid his arms around my waist.

"Mmmm..." I said as he kissed my neck. He pulled me hard toward him. I could feel his hard-on on my ass. His hands slowly slid up under my shirt, and he squeezed my breasts through my bra. He kept kissing my neck.

"I can't take it anymore," he said, moving his hands back to my waist and turning me around. "Let's go." He guided me inside, back to the bedroom. We stood at the foot of the bed, kissing, tongues playing.

I grabbed his ass and said, "I owe you." I turned him away from the bed and pushed him onto it. I climbed on top of him as he unbuttoned my shirt and unclasped my bra.

"That's what I'm talkin' about," he said as my breasts swung free. I laughed and unbuttoned his shirt. Next I undid his belt and pants and got up to pull them off from the cuffs.

True to form, his underwear didn't disappoint. Boxer briefs again, this time dark blue and skintight. He caught his breath at my touch when I stroked his dick and balls through the fabric. Ah, but as sexy as they were, his briefs had to come off for what I had in mind.

I thought of something. I crawled back on top of him and kissed him. "Make yourself comfortable; I'll be right back."

He groaned. "Are you kidding me?"

"Just relax." I climbed back down and headed to the kitchen, where I found a glass and dispensed some ice. I headed back to the bedroom, picked a tie up off the floor, and crawled back on him. He'd moved up on the bed. I took the tie and laid it over his eyes.

"Ooo, I like where this is going," he said.

"Oh, you'll like it all right." I tied the tie behind his head and reached for the glass. I took an ice cube out and sucked it. I took it out of my mouth and held it above his nipple. I let it drip.

He jumped. "Aahhh!"

When I touched his nipple with the tip of the ice cube, he yelped again. His nipple stood at attention. I moved to the other nipple and touched the ice to it. "Mmmm," he said, pushing his chest toward me. I stroked his nipple with the ice. He held his breath. I gave his other nipple the same treatment before I slid the ice down his chest to his happy trail. I held the dripping cube over his dick. He jumped at the first drop, and the second.

My ice cube was getting too wet, so I got another one and rolled it around my mouth. I took it out and clamped my mouth around the head.

"Oh God! What are ya doing?"

I giggled, sliding my mouth up and down him, pausing for more ice as it melted. I ran my finger up his ass crack. He caught his breath. I held an ice cube in my hand, dropped it in the glass, and grasped his shaft, still sucking the head. He propelled himself into my mouth, and I grabbed another ice cube—they were all wet by now—and touched between his dick and ass, traced it around a little as he let out a moan. I dropped it back in the glass and stuck my finger up his ass as I continued to pump. "Oh!" He thrust harder. I kept sucking, pumping, and playing in his ass until he grabbed the blindfold, took it off, and said, "That's it. I've gotta fuck you!"

He grabbed a condom, ripped it open, and put it on. He motioned to me. "On your knees." I complied, and he positioned himself behind me and spread my ass cheeks. My body spasmed as he pushed himself deep into me. He grabbed my waist and said, "Come on up." He held my waist as I walked my hands up the headboard to a kneeling position.

He grabbed my breasts and drove himself deeper into me. He kept pumping as he moved one hand down to my aching clit. I jumped when he touched it. My loins got hot, and my nipples stood at attention. I wanted more. His dick hit my G-spot, and I held my breath, trying to come. He kept the rest of his hand still as he stroked my clit. I felt the tingling and the heat as spasms rocked my pussy, and I squeezed him as he continued to thrust. I was still coming when I heard him strain and grunt, and then I felt him jerk inside me.

He held my breasts and supported me. He lay on my back for a second, hugging me, before his dick pulled out. His weight gently pushed me back to my hands and knees. He flopped on the bed, and I lay down next to him. His forehead was still sweating, and he was out of breath. "Oh my God," he huffed. "That was huge."

I smiled and kissed him. "You're welcome."

He lay there, catching his breath. Then he reached for me and pulled me to him. I put my head on his still-damp chest. He said, "I was thinking about you all day."

"Me too."

"I knew that this would be great but not this great."

I smiled. "Glad to be of service."

"You're amazing."

"You're not so bad yourself."

We lay there awhile. "Let me go take this off," he said, pinching the condom and heading for the bathroom.

"Hey," I called. "Do you remember what I was supposed to do for that meeting?"

"Me."

"I'll check that one off. No, they gave me something. Do you even know what the meeting was about?"

He came back in the room. "Nope. Do you?" He climbed into bed.

"Nope. You distracted me."

He raised his eyebrows, giving me an innocent look. "I did?"

I rolled over onto his chest. "Especially when you bit my leg. What was that?"

"It blocked my view when I tried to look up your skirt."

I laughed. "Dammit, I'll have to ask Melissa what they told me to do. I hope she knows, or I'm gonna have to call Wind-Power Jennifer, and that'll be embarrassing."

"You didn't seem to mind the distraction in the elevator."

I raised my eyebrows. "I didn't mind the distraction in the elevator."

"I figured that when you came. And I didn't."

"Well, what did you wanna do, cream your pants? Which, by the way, show off that gorgeous ass very well." I gave him a lascivious look.

"Thank you. I told you what I wanted to do. Go to a hotel."

I shook my head slowly. "Yeah. Nick. That was not gonna happen in the middle of the day. You're the boss at your work, but I am not the boss at mine. My boss expects me to show up."

"We're gonna do it. You get a lunch, don't you?"

I nodded. "Yeah, but it wasn't lunchtime."

"But it will be, someday, and we'll book a hotel room."

It *would* be hot. "I have no problem with that. I just need to know in advance."

"Fair enough. I'll send you a meeting invite. You hungry?"

"Famished."

"Lemme get the menus." He got up and went to the kitchen; when he returned, he sat up in bed. I got up to join him. "We've got Chinese, barbecue, sushi, Mexican—"

"Ooo, I love the sushi place here."

"Sushi it is." He handed me the menu. "Let me get a pen."

When he brought it, I marked off a dragon roll and some nigiri. He took a pass at it and called. I watched his arm flex as he held the phone and studied his chest. How did I wind up here with Nick Martone? And the way he was acting—like he liked me—that was the weird part. I still didn't trust it. He said that stuff about falling for women, but how long could a guy like him last with one person?

"OK, coming." He tackled me on the bed, kissed me as I giggled, and rolled on his side next to me. "You're staying the night, right?"

When did "stay" stop being a question and become a statement? At least I was prepared. "Yes, I am. All that shopping was for clothes for tomorrow."

"Good." He slapped the bed. Little-kid mode. "Come closer."

I shifted over. He kissed me, gave me a big grin, and kissed me, while giving me a big hug. Little-kid mode was fun.

"I guess we should get dressed," I said, moving to get up.

He reached out and pulled me back down. "No, we shouldn't!" We kissed some more.

"Is the delivery guy from the sushi place in love with you, too?" I teased.

"I certainly hope so! Then I can skimp on the tip."

I laughed. "Man, if you'd seen what I saw in the hotel room. I thought the guy was about to go all gay porn on you."

Nick let out a loud laugh and made his voice deep. "Special de-*liv*-ery, sir..."

"Oh, I don't have a tip..."

"You don't need money with *me*, sir..." He hummed porn music.

I tried to stop laughing. "Sounds like you've seen your share of gay porn."

"I'll never tell." Nice that he was comfortable with his sexuality. At least he wasn't one of these guys who sleeps around just to prove he's not the least bit bisexual.

The buzzer rang, and Nick jumped up, put on shorts, and buzzed the delivery guy in. I rooted around for my clothes. I heard Nick answer the door, talk to the delivery guy, thank him, and then close the door. "You ready?" he called to the bedroom.

"I'll be right there." I zipped up my skirt.

We ate at the table. Nick had a bottle of plum wine, so we drank that with our sushi. We exchanged bites and stories, flirted and laughed. God, I was so comfortable with him. Then again, how could I not be after all the sex we'd had?

After dinner, we watched *Family Guy* while cuddled on the couch. At bedtime, he gave me a T-shirt to sleep in, and we spooned until we were ready to sleep. We kissed good night, and I rolled over.

In the morning, we took turns taking showers—thankfully because I didn't think I could take anymore sex just yet. He was already in khakis and a bowling shirt as he watched me get dressed. I felt awkward, but he came over to button my shirt and gave me a sweet kiss. "So we're on for Saturday?"

I hadn't had coffee yet. "Saturday?"

"Yeah, dinner at your place?"

Hell, yes. "Oh right, it *is* Saturday. Sorry. Yes, we're on."

"Seven?"

"Yeah, seven's good."

We walked to the Metro together and squeezed ourselves onto a train. We were more intimate with the passengers that morning than we'd been with each other. The Orange Line fills up at the very first stop. Ours was the fifth. Thankfully, my work was only two stops away. When we got there, Nick got off the train with me.

"What are you doing?"

"Saying good-bye."

That was fucking crazy. "*Here?*"

"I'm not gonna see you for days!" he whined.

"Nick, my coworkers get off at this stop."

"Nobody's gonna see us. Come on!" It was a losing battle. He took my hand and led me to the wall, steering me against it. "I'll even stand in front of you so nobody sees you."

"They know you too!"

"Would you relax, woman?" He took my face in his hands and kissed me softly. He parted his lips, and our tongues played a little. I stifled a sound. We broke; he gave me one more soft kiss and said, "See you Saturday."

"See you Saturday," I said. He walked back across the platform. I watched as another packed train arrived, a few people got off, and he fought his way on.

5

Meeting Offline

When I logged onto my computer, there was an e-mail from Melissa.

Are you free for lunch?

She wanted the dirt on Nick, and I was happy to have someone to share it with, so we made plans. The morning dragged, but lunchtime came eventually, and I left to meet Melissa at the restaurant. We usually met at the Indian buffet between our offices. When I got there, she was waiting. I sat down at the table.

"Hey, hi. How are you?"

The busboy filled up my water. "Good, good."

"So, what's going on with Nick?"

"Let's get food before I start. If we don't, we'll never eat."

When we were back at the table, she said, "OK, spill it. How'd you meet?"

I started to tell the story.

"You slept with him the first night? You slut!" Melissa joked. "How's he hung?"

"Pretty well, actually. Average length but above average girth."

"That's all that counts. How many times have you done the deed?"

"Five."

"Since last Wednesday?"

"Yep."

"I'd heard he was a stud, but even Jason can't do that." She really was having trouble with monogamy.

"There's something about the two of us. It's this incredible chemistry."

"And you think he likes you?" she asked skeptically.

"Thanks for the vote of confidence."

"Come on, Angie. You know who he is."

"Yeah, and that's the problem. I know exactly who he is, but he does all this sweet stuff, and he tells me I'm different than the other women."

"And you buy that?"

"Sometimes. I do have a hard time believing him, though. I mean he's shown me that he's trustworthy; it's just his reputation."

"Once a player, always a player."

"I guess so."

"But hey, you're getting laid, and pretty damn well, it sounds like."

"Very. Very. Well."

"So enjoy it while it lasts. You don't need to marry him."

I sighed. "Yeah, you're right. Speaking of marriage, how are the wedding plans coming?"

My phone buzzed on my way back to the office. I had a voice mail: *Hey, it's Nick. Can you send me your address, sexy?*

Melissa was right. Sexy. Not sweetie, not honey, not even beautiful. Just sexy. That was what he was thinking. But hell, the sex was unbelievable. When I got back to my desk, I e-mailed him my address.

You didn't tell me you lived so close. See you tomorrow, gorgeous.

Sex again.

I e-mailed back: *Can't wait.*

I was wet just typing.

It was raining when I woke up Saturday. Nice day for cooking, but I still had to shop for ingredients. I headed up to the Italian Store on Lee Highway and picked up crushed tomatoes, some pasta, grated Romano cheese, and some cannoli for dessert. I'd thought about starting my gravy from fresh tomatoes, but tomatoes take forever to cook down, and I couldn't be sure the gravy would be ready in time. Plus I had to cook the meatballs in it, so it had to be done way before dinner.

The canned tomatoes bought me a little time. I wanted to feel confident, so I went for a short run, showered, changed, and started my gravy. I decided to make my own pasta. Maybe it wasn't the best occasion for my first time, but dammit, I'd had that pasta attachment for my KitchenAid for a long time and never used it; plus I had all day *and* backup pasta, in case it didn't work.

I went to work on the pasta dough. I wished I had Nick's kitchen because I didn't have a lot of room on my Formica counter. As I measured for it, I thought about Nick and the little things he did. The hand holding, kissing at the train station, asking to hear so much about me. If he didn't like me, why would he do those things? Was that just part of his charm? The sex was good enough to keep me coming back without bringing feelings into it. And the thing was, he was so sweet when we were together. But somebody who was that much of a player could fake that, right? Right? I was better off being cautious. So why was I making my own damn pasta? I didn't mind cooking. I never got to cook for anybody, so it was fun. But it would be more fun if the romance was real.

The pasta seemed to come out fine, but I wouldn't know until I cooked it, and that was later. I made meatballs, baked them, and put them aside to wait for the gravy to cook. I'd worked up a sweat, so I went to take another shower and pick out clothes.

Lathering up, I thought about that shower we took together. Man, that was hot! How the hell did he do it? He'd just come in bed when we woke up. Comes with the player territory, I guess. Melissa was right. I couldn't get involved. I'd only get hurt.

After my shower, I threw on sweats and popped the meatballs into the gravy. I let it all simmer while I straightened up the apartment. His apartment was pretty tidy when I saw it. He must have a maid. Either that or he straightened up for me, and guys don't do that just to get laid. Stop it, Angie! Stop it!

About twenty minutes before our date, I got dressed and made sure my mascara wasn't running and my lipstick was fresh. I plugged my iPod into the dock and played my 1940s playlist. I lowered the burner on the gravy to warm and set the pasta pot to low so it would warm up fast when I wanted it to.

The buzzer rang, and I buzzed him in. I had butterflies.

Really, Angie? For a guy who's just a lay? But what a lay!

I heard the knock and opened the door. He was holding a shopping bag and a huge bouquet of roses.

"Hi," he said, giving me a quick kiss. He held out the roses. "These are for you."

"Thank you!"

"I finally got the chance to get you flowers."

"They're beautiful! And huge! Didja get 'em at Costco or something?"

"I owed you a dozen from our first date. And another for today."

"Lemme put them in water."

He peeked in the gravy pot. "Gravy? Man, Greek girl who can cook Italian. Seriously, you just get better and better!"

I laughed.

"Can I help with something?"

"You can open the wine." I rooted in the drawers and handed him a corkscrew.

"I'm surprised you went Italian. I thought you were gonna go all Greek on me."

"Is that a double entendre?"

"Only if you want it to be." He winked at me over the wine bottle.

"I walked right into that one."

He grinned. "Backward."

"Yeah, just so you know, that's not really my thing."

He changed the subject. "Wineglasses?"

I pointed to the glass cabinet.

He came up behind me and circled his arms around my waist. "I believe I've got your things pretty well covered."

He felt so good against me. He kissed my neck. I turned around and kissed him. My whole lower half tingled. He opened his mouth and played with my tongue and kissed my lips on the way out. He turned around, grabbed two wineglasses, finished opening the bottle, poured, and handed me one. "To a Greek girl who cooks Italian."

I laughed and clinked my glass to his.

"So what didja do all day?" he asked.

"Whaddaya think? I made gravy."

"I'm sorry. I didn't mean to make you cook all day."

"No, it's OK. I had fun. Plus I needed gravy to freeze."

"Didja make the meatballs?"

"Of course, I made the meatballs. What kind of Italian cook do you think I am? And the pasta. I made the pasta."

"From scratch? Seriously?"

"I had this pasta attachment for my KitchenAid, and I wanted to use it. If it comes out bad, I have store-bought for backup."

"I'm sure it'll be fantastic. Wow, I didn't mean to put you to work."

He didn't? "Greek would have been work. This was fun."

"And we're back to Greek. Are you trying to tell me something?"

"So now it's a double entendre." I lifted my glass in salute.

He came closer and held my waist. "I will never ask you to do something you don't want to do."

"Ah, but there's so much I wanna do! Hey, do you like olives?"

"Come on, I'm Greek and Italian."

"Stupid question. I was gonna make antipasto, but I thought it would be too much, so I just bought some olives."

"I didn't mean for you to go all out."

I shrugged. "I'm an all-out kind of girl."

"I didn't know that."

"There's a lot you don't know."

"I'm dying to find out."

Was this a guy who wasn't interested? Shut up, Angie, I thought. You knew he was a snake when you picked him up. Don't let yourself get hurt. Out loud, I just said, "Good thing we're having dinner."

"Speaking of dinner, what else can I do to help?"

We munched olives while he made the garlic bread. I cooked the pasta and tasted it. "I think it's fine. What do you think?" I asked, holding up a strand, while realizing I could have done a test strand before I cooked the whole batch. Oh, well.

He came over, and I dangled the strand above his mouth. He tilted his head back and bit. "Yeah, it's great! Have you ever made it before?"

"Nope."

"You're pretty amazing."

"You're just saying that 'cause you're hungry."

"Well, I meant it, but I *am* hungry."

I was draining the pasta. "We're almost ready." I dumped the linguini back in the pot and ladled some gravy into it, stirring. "Can you put the cheese on the table?"

I grabbed two pasta bowls, portioned the pasta, added meatballs, and we were ready. I put both bowls on the table, and we sat down.

"A toast," Nick said, holding up his glass. "To an all-out kind of girl."

"You're embarrassing me, but what the hell. Cheers!"

He took a bite, chewed. "Oh my God, Angie!" he said. "This is unbelievable."

"Thanks. I think I'm a better Italian cook than Greek."

"We'll have to do a comparison."

I laughed. "OK. What's your favorite Greek food?"

"I'd have to say souvlaki. But with lamb. Not that stupid chicken that the Greek places all sell."

"Oh boy, are you in luck! My *thia* handed down the most amazing souvlaki recipe. I'll have to make it for you sometime."

Now I was making future plans. Dammit, Angie!

"If it's half as good as your linguini and meatballs, I'm all over it."

"I don't have a grill, though."

"You can make it at my place. Grills on the balconies are strictly frowned upon, but I can get away with a hibachi from time to time."

"That would be great. I love having an excuse to make souvlaki."

"I love giving you one. And I have to take you out to thank you for this."

"Hmm, that's not what I was expecting..."

"That too. Seriously, though I wanna take you out."

"I can't do that, Nick. DC is such a small town. What if we run into somebody we know?"

Nick shook his head. "What if we go someplace the people in our circle can't afford?"

"How do you know what they can afford?"

"Oh, I know. I hand out the funding, remember? I do see financials."

"I guess we could do that."

His body relaxed. "Good. It's settled."

"So when we went to dinner, you asked me what I do for fun. What do you do?"

"I play softball on the mall. I bike. I take myself to the museums."

"I used to play softball on the mall, but I left my old job and couldn't play for the team anymore. What position do you play?"

"Short."

"Nice. Are you any good?"

"Come, see me play, and I'll show you."

"Maybe I will."

He raised one eyebrow. "You're not worried about running into anybody?"

"Why? It's not like nonprofits have the cash to field softball teams."

"No."

"Well, there ya go." Oddly enough, you never ran into anybody on the mall, even though everybody went. It had to be the expanse that kept everyone from bumping into each other. "What's your favorite museum?"

"I think I'd have to say Natural History."

"I like the bug exhibit there, but for me, nothing will ever compare to Natural History in New York."

"Which one's your favorite?"

"American History. You just can't beat Oscar the Grouch and Fonzie's jacket."

"Good point. I like American History. I'd love to take you there."

That again? Come on, Angie, he's just being nice. "Yeah, maybe." I changed the subject. "So what was it like working for Greenpeace?"

"Just a stupid thing after college. At first, I was one of those annoying people who stop you on the sidewalk to do surveys and ask for money. But I didn't feel that I was really doing anything, so I signed up to fight whaling."

"So you were one of those people in the little rafts?"

"Yep. And let me tell ya, when you're on an inflatable with a two-hundred-ton whaling ship on one side and a twenty-five-ton whale on the other, you're shitting your pants."

"Did you stop a lot of whaling?"

"Oh no, they don't give a shit. They just do their thing, and they don't care if they kill you."

"Did anybody die?"

"No, fortunately, but I decided that Greenpeace wasn't for me. So I went back home and talked about moving to DC to do something environmental. My uncle took me aside, and we came up with the idea for the Green Trust. I had a minor in finance, so it was perfect."

"What was your major?"

"Environmental science."

"Environmental science and finance. That's a weird combination."

"It was a compromise. My parents wanted me to study something that would get me a good job."

"And here you are."

"Yep. Man, I'm full, but it's so good, I want to eat more."

"I know the feeling." Great, call attention to your gigantic appetite.

"Dinner was amazing, Angie. Thanks."

"You're welcome. I bought cannoli too."

"Really? Hopefully I can squeeze one in later. After I've worked up an appetite."

"Oh, and how do you expect to do that?"

"You'll see. In the meantime, let me do the dishes, at least. You did so much. Relax for a while."

"OK, you can just get them in the dishwasher. I'll put the meatballs away."

"I can do it; just tell me where the Tupperware is."

"The cabinet next to the stove."

"Got it. Sit." I went over to the couch and lit some candles. I realized my lipstick would have worn off and went to the bathroom to fix it.

"Sit, I said!"

"Just going to powder my nose."

He was just finishing up when I got out. "Should I run the dishwasher?" he asked.

"No, it's loud. I'll run it later."

"OK." We met in the living room. "It Had to Be You" was playing. He held out his hand. "May I have this dance?"

I giggled. "Dance?"

"Yeah, this music is great for slow dancing."

I took his hand and rested the other on his shoulder. It felt good to be in his arms. Still, sparks buzzed between us. My nipples hardened, and I felt myself lube up, anticipating.

"You know all those restaurants that people go to on TV, where there's a dance floor and a jazz band, so they can dance after dinner? I wish they really existed," I said.

"If I find one, I'll take you."

"Mmmm." I reached up to him, and he gave me a sweet kiss. We kept dancing.

He kissed me again, and I couldn't wait. I opened my mouth and played with his tongue. He slid his hands down to the small of my back and pulled me close. He tickled my tongue, and I couldn't take anymore. I led him to the couch. We sat down and kissed some more as he pushed me down on my back and got on top of me, slipping his hands under my shirt.

I broke our kiss. "Let's get on the floor. I don't want a wet spot on the couch."

His eyes smiled. "Oh, were you planning on making a wet spot?" He got up, and we settled on the rug.

"I was a Girl Scout. I have to be prepared."

We kissed some more, and he pulled my shirt up and over my head. "You too," I said, taking off his shirt. He kissed me again, and then he slid his hands under my back and unhooked my bra. He pulled it over my arms and whispered, "I couldn't wait for this." He leaned on his side and took one breast in his hand, caressing and pinching the nipple. He took the other breast in his mouth, sucking and licking. My whole body went on alert. I moaned and arched my back. He slid his hand into my pants, under my panties, and felt my wet pussy. Finally! I moaned, arching my back again.

"You're so wet," he said, exploring me with his fingers. He moved down to my pants, unbuttoned and unzipped, and pulled them off me. He bit my mound lightly, teasing, before he pulled off my panties. I took my breast in my hand and played with my nipple as he slowly and sparsely teased my clit with his finger.

He took my other hand in his and guided it down to my clit. "Play with it," he said, "for me. I wanna see you make yourself come."

"Mmmm," I said, massaging around and on my hardened clit and playing with my nipple while he watched. His focus on my pussy made me so hot. I kept stroking as I watched his eyes wander up to my nipple and back down. I slid my finger down, caressing my lower lips. I couldn't take my eyes off Nick, practically drooling over this show. I stroked some more, but I wanted it so bad that my hand gravitated toward my clit. My body stiffened.

"No, not yet," he said. "Slowly."

I followed his instruction and rubbed around my clit and right below it. I kept my hand moving, letting it wander down to my hole. I arched my back as I fingered myself. Nick's eyes focused on my pussy. I couldn't take it anymore. I slid my fingers along my lips as slowly as I could, but I had to go in for the kill. I flicked my clit, harder, and kept going as I felt the orgasm build. I looked at him watching me again and kept stroking. I held my breath as I came, arching my back. I felt the hot liquid run down my lips as I squirted.

"More?" he said.

"No," I said, breathless, shaking my head.

"Good." He got out of his jeans and briefs, fumbled in his pocket for a condom, found it, ripped it open, and put it on. He crawled up to me, lifted my open legs over his, and found my hole. My pussy was still spasming from the orgasm as he pushed into me. I loved the way he filled me up and that he was in me while I was out of control. "That was so hot!" he said, pumping. I just lay back and enjoyed it for a while.

When my body caught its breath, I lifted my pelvis to meet him, and I squeezed him. I reached up and played with his nipples, and he groaned. I slid my hands to his arms, feeling the contours of his muscles. I squeezed him again, and he pumped faster, his face screwing up. I held his arms as I strained to meet him, making myself as tight as possible and grunting as he thrust into me. His face screwed up more, and he stopped pumping. I felt the spasms inside of me. They kept going as his body jerked, and he collapsed on top of me. "Oh God, that was great," he huffed as he kissed me. He carefully extracted himself and lay down next to me. "That was so hot!"

It was hot. "Glad you liked it," I said as he rolled over, resting his head on my breast. He traced his finger down my chest. "Are you busy tomorrow?"

"Not really. I was gonna take a walk and get some stuff done around the house."

"Can I stay?"

"Yeah, I was just gonna ask you."

"Good."

"Lemme go get rid of this," he said, indicating the used condom.

"Yeah, so much for my rug," I said as I watched him walk to the bathroom.

"That was you," he called out.

"I know."

"Nothing a little Resolve can't fix," he said.

"And you know this from experience?"

"I spill a lot of stuff."

"Oh." I got up and headed to the bedroom. "Meet you in here, OK?" I said, hesitating at the bathroom.

"Be right there." The toilet flushed. "Hey, do you have an extra toothbrush?"

I gasped. "You didn't bring one?"

"I didn't want to presume."

"Yeah, look in the medicine cabinet." I pulled back the covers on the bed. It was gonna be nice having someone to share it.

Nick came out of the bathroom. "I'm gonna get my clothes."

"I'm gonna brush my teeth," I said and went to the bathroom. When I came out, Nick was lying on my bed in just his briefs, his clothes folded neatly on the chair. I got a nightshirt out of my drawer and joined him.

"Which side is yours?" he asked.

Neither. "Hmm, I guess you can take that side."

"OK. Roll over." I did, and he sidled up and spooned me. Oh yes, it was gonna be nice having someone share my bed. "You know, you never gave me a tour of your apartment."

"Well, you saw the kitchen, the living room, the bathroom, and here. That's pretty much it."

"I like what you've done with the place."

"Oh, my friend Kim helped me with that. She's got a really good eye for decorating." Kim had helped me turn yard sale special into shabby chic, for the most part. My living-room couch was decent discount furniture, but everything else was a collection of interesting but serendipitous finds and various framed posters.

"It's still very you. I like it."

"Thank you."

"Good night." He kissed my neck.

"Good night."

I woke up to noises in my house, which freaked me out, until I smelled bacon and I remembered that Nick stayed over. I wandered out into the kitchen.

"Good morning, sleepyhead," he said.

"Good morning." There were two mugs of coffee on my kitchen table. "What are ya doing?"

"Cooking breakfast."

"I thought you didn't cook."

"I'm a gentleman. I know how to make breakfast for a lady."

"Of course, you do."

"I'm gonna ignore that. Siddown. I'm almost done."

"It smells great."

"Blame it on the bacon." He went for two plates, scooped eggs into them, and put three slices of bacon on each. "Here you are, beautiful." He kissed me. "And thank you for last night." He set the plate at my place and settled himself across from me.

I looked down at my plate. "You made Greek eggs?"

"Yeah, I thought you'd appreciate them. I hope you weren't saving that feta and tomato for anything."

"Nope. Nothing in particular. This is great, Nick! And the bacon's perfect!"

"I'm glad you like it." He winked. "So when do I take you out to thank you for dinner?"

"Uh, I don't know."

"Don't worry. We'll go somewhere no one will see us, although I don't get what the big deal is with you."

I brought a forkful of eggs to my lips, but then set it down again. "My reputation is the big deal."

"Why? You're a grown woman; you can sleep with anyone you want to. This isn't high school. You don't have to worry about a reputation."

"See, you've got nothing to lose. You can be seen with anybody. You're the playboy. You're the guy with the money. You're in the power position. I have to consider my reputation."

"Again, you're a grown woman. Why is that a problem?" Nick seemed genuinely perplexed as he munched a piece of bacon.

"It's not about that. It's about my business reputation. If people in our business see me with you, number one, they'll think I fell for your act, and number two, if you fund Hydrogen Futures at all, I'll look like a whore."

"So I guess I just won't give you guys a grant."

"That makes it even worse. Then my boss is mad at me for fucking our funding up. It never ends."

"Let's get back to 'my act.' What's 'my act'?"

"You know, charming, flirtatious, leading me on."

"I'm leading you on? How am I leading you on? And who says 'leading on' anymore? This is the millennium."

"By acting like you care about me."

"I do care about you. Haven't I shown you that?"

I shrugged. "You've shown me a lot of things."

"What's that supposed to mean?"

"You're sweet; you seem interested in me, and you always make plans, but we always wind up in bed together."

"First of all, I *seem* interested? You think I *seem* interested just to get you into bed? And you're saying you don't want to sleep with me? Maybe it's *your* act, but you seem pretty willing."

"I am willing to sleep with you. But it's the other stuff. I don't know, Nick. How am I supposed to trust someone with your reputation?"

"I thought we were past that."

"I guess we're not."

He came over, kneeled beside me, and gently turned me to face him, holding my shoulders. "Look, Angie. I like you. I really do. And I'll do what it takes to prove it to you, but I can't do that until you're willing to trust me."

"I just. I just don't wanna invest myself in this and then get hurt."

"That is the last thing I ever want to do. I promise you that. OK?" He kissed me.

"OK."

"So when are we going out?"

"Next weekend, I guess. You wear me out way too much for during the week."

Nick shook his head. "Oh no, I can't wait that long. I need to wear you out before then."

"Yeah, but we don't have to go out during the week."

"Fair enough. We go out next weekend. But we get together this week."

I couldn't wait a week either. "Yeah, sure. This week."

"Are you OK this morning? Do you need to go back to bed?"

"Shut up," I said.

"I'm just worried you're worn out."

"You didn't do much to wear me out last night." I raised one eyebrow.

"But I loved what you did to yourself. Or are you saying I owe you?"

"I'll let you know."

"You sure you don't wanna go back to bed?"

I raised the other eyebrow. "I'm sensing a theme here."

He took my hands, pulled me up, and put his arms around me. "This"—he kissed me—"is the theme." He sank those soft lips onto mine, slowly.

"I like this theme." I kissed him back.

"Let's get a little more comfortable." He took my hand and led me back to the bedroom; the rest of breakfast sat on the table, getting cold.

6

Business Lunch

Monday morning I got an instant message from Nick: *Hi, cutie.* I responded: *Hi.*

Nick Martone: *Thinking about you. I had a really great time over the weekend.*

Me: *Me too.*

Nick Martone: *Can I take you to lunch?*

Me: *In public?*

Nick Martone: *Georgetown. Nobody we know goes there.*

Me: *I guess so.*

Nick Martone: *Don't sound so enthused.*

Me: *No, I wanna see you; I just have to be careful.*

Nick Martone: *How's tomorrow?*

Me: *Tomorrow's good.*

Nick Martone: *The Woods at 12:30?*

Me: *OK, meet you there.*

Nick Martone: *See ya, cutie.*
Me: *See ya then, sexy.*

I put my face in my hands. Lunch? Was he gonna want to go to lunch all the time? Shit. Granted, no one we knew hung out in Georgetown, but no matter how discreet we were, we'd run into someone someday. This city was such a small town. Still, I missed him.

On Tuesday, I took a cab to Georgetown. It doesn't have a Metro stop, and it would've been a long walk—especially in work shoes. I got there before him, and the host walked me outside to a table in the shade. The big trees framed the view of the Potomac so well, and the restaurant was filled with beautiful people. I had some time to think.

What was I gonna tell him about lunches? If I didn't say something, he'd start asking me all the time, and I'd have to say no. And he'd get offended. I didn't want to hurt his feelings.

I saw him at the door, wearing a white button-down shirt and tie. Our eyes locked as the host walked him over to me.

He leaned over to kiss me. "Hi."

"Hi."

He sat down. "You look beautiful."

I noticed his tie had little blue sailboats on it. "You look great too."

He picked up his menu. "How's work?"

"It's OK. Doing a lot of research, going to a couple of hearings this week. You?"

"Reading proposals all day. I've got three hundred K that I've got to award."

I put on a serious face. "That's really rough. How do you handle it?"

He laughed. "I get by."

The waiter came by and took our drink order.

I slipped my shoe off and reached for his ankle. "So, what's new? What's going on?"

He twitched at my touch. "Ooo, so that's how this lunch is gonna be."

I looked innocent. "Just a little flirting. Is that a problem?"

"Not at all." He smiled. "This morning I booked a trip to Massachusetts to check out some wave-energy sites."

"Really? When?"

"Next week."

"For how long?"

"A week."

A week? He was leaving me for a week? I couldn't go three days without him, and he was leaving for a week?

I took a deep breath and tried to stay neutral. "Well, it's a nice time of year for Massachusetts. Are you gonna be near the Cape?"

"I'll be driving up and down the coast, including out on the Cape."

"You could go out to Martha's Vineyard or Nantucket over the weekend."

Over the weekend? Did I just say that? Neutral, Angie. Don't convince him to stay longer!

"I may take a ferry ride, but I won't be spending the weekend there. I'm leaving on Sunday and coming back on Friday. Besides," he said, picking up his glass, "I wouldn't want to go to those places without you."

Oh my God, Nick, good answer. Still, that's almost seven days without him! Shit! OK, I could say it. "I'm gonna miss you."

He leaned in and held my hand. "I'm gonna miss you too."

I played with his ankle while we looked at our menus. He kept looking up to smile at me. The waiter took our order, and we talked about work and play and plans.

He reminded me of a meeting we had on Friday. "Are you going?" he said.

"I'm supposed to. Is it gonna be anything like the last meeting?"

He frowned. "I don't know what you mean by that."

"Oh, you're funny. Are you gonna sit next to me and play footsie under the table?"

"Coming from someone who's got her foot up my pants, that seems like a strange question."

I withdrew my foot. "I'm sorry; I was looking for my shoe."

He gave me a sly smile. "If you don't want me to sit next to you—I mean, if it's too distracting—I can keep my distance."

Oh, you wish! "Don't run away on my account."

The waiter brought my grilled chicken and his burger and coleslaw.

He tented his fingers in evil-genius fashion. "I see. But what if our esteemed colleagues notice we're sitting together again?"

I knew they wouldn't notice. "I'll take that chance."

He leaned forward. "Of course. You *were* the one who benefited from that meeting."

"You benefited too. You just had to wait a few hours."

"A hell of a few hours."

"Look, sit with me; don't sit with me. You've got to do what's best for you." I smiled.

"I'll give it some serious thought."

"You're so full of shit."

He pointed his fork at my food. "How's yours?"

"It's good. It's as good as a grilled chicken sandwich can be."

"No one orders grilled chicken unless they're dieting. Woman, are you dieting now? You do *not* need to diet. You're perfect the way you are."

"You're really sweet, you know that?"

He smiled serenely. "I am, aren't I?"

"You really are."

"So when's our next date, Angie?"

"Oh, well, depending on what you decide to do at the meeting, we may need one on Friday."

"You know if we get a hotel room at lunch, I won't have to touch you at the meeting."

"Not gonna happen. Friday's fairly busy for me. For a Friday during the summer."

"OK, Friday night it is. Where do you wanna go?"

"Your place? Otherwise I'll have to clean."

"My place it is. Seven?"

"Seven's good."

I walked to the Foggy Bottom Metro on the way back. I figured my feet could take a one-way trip. It was a beautiful day, and I hadn't spent enough time outside. Plus every time I saw Nick, I needed some equivalent of a cold shower. As I approached the Metro stop, I realized we never discussed the "no more lunches" thing. I had never met anybody with his ability to throw me off my game.

Later that afternoon, I got an instant message.

> Nick Martone: *You drove me crazy. I tried to be a gentleman, but I can't take it any longer. I have to see you.*
> Excellent. I answered: *OK, my place after work?*
> Nick Martone: *I'll be there with balls—oops,* bells—*on.*
> Me: *See you later.*

Truth be told, I was having a hard time seeing him without the prospect of sex. Well, problem solved.

I had picked up my apartment a little, but I wasn't home long before I buzzed Nick in. He got to my door in seconds. When I let him in, he took my face in his hands and kissed me, and kissed me, and kissed me. It was all I could do to get the door closed. He reached down to my legs and lifted them. I wrapped my legs around his waist.

How could he just lift me like that? I didn't think his arms were *that* strong.

He broke our kiss. "I have to have you," he breathed. "I just have to be inside you. It's all I could think about all day. Can we just...? Right now?"

I'd never seen him like this. "Yeah, yeah, we can."

He put me down on the bed and unbuttoned his pants. I started to take mine off too. He had his pants off and condom on before I could get my pants over my ankles.

He reached for my shoulders. "Right now."

I spread my legs. Still standing, he plunged himself in, pumping hard and fast. My body was on high alert. The rhythm was welcome, but it wasn't enough for me. Still, the intensity on his face showed me how much he needed to come. I let my breath go, moaning as he pushed. I squeezed and squeezed until I saw his face screw up. He cried out as he came, thrusting all the way into me. He held himself there for the after-shocks. He leaned down to me and hugged me. "Thank you."

"You're welcome. Are you OK?"

He took a deep breath. "Yeah. I'm OK now...I just had to have you... I couldn't get my mind off you today." He rested on top of me.

"Are you sure you're OK? I've never seen you like that."

"I'm sorry. I just got so worked up. I wanted you so badly. I don't think I've ever been that way before. I'm sorry."

"You don't have to be sorry. I just wanted to know what was going on with you."

He kissed me and pointed at the condom. "Let me go get this thing off, and I'll make it up to you."

"OK," I said as he got up. My body was still anticipating sex. My nipples were like bullets, and everything else was engorged and looking for relief.

Nick came back to the bed and started to undress me. "I can see the high beams. Let's see what they look like underneath."

"Mmmm." I smiled at him, and he kissed me, pulled my shirt apart, and brushed my nipples through my bra.

He reached his hand inside my bra and freed that breast and then the other. "Very nice." He tweaked my nipple. "You could cut glass with this."

I laughed, enjoying the tingles he sent through my body.

He pinched my nipples in little pulses. I arched my back and moaned.

He stopped. "I was thinking we could do something a little different. Do you have any toys?"

Hmm, OK. I was ready. "In that drawer." I pointed at the bedside table.

He crawled up to my nightstand and opened the drawer. "Nice col-lection. I can definitely work with these." He pulled out my vibrator. "The Rabbit. Excellent choice." Next came a little egg-shaped vibrator. "Oh, I have plans for this already." He pulled out a vibrating cock ring but then dropped it back in the drawer. "Hmm, I'll keep this in mind for the future. OK, some lube and we're ready."

He turned the Rabbit on vibrate and touched it to my pussy lips. I immediately wanted to come. I felt like I'd been waiting so long. He traced the Rabbit around my lips, never touching my clit. He kept doing it, driving me crazy. He touched the Rabbit's ears to my clit for a second, and I jumped, but he pulled it away and teased me some more.

"Let's try this one," he said, holding the silver egg up so I could see it. He took the Rabbit away for a second and pushed the egg all the way into me. The vibrations inside started a whole new orgasm building; then he touched the Rabbit's ears to my lips, and I moaned and writhed. I didn't think I could take anymore, but he backed off and turned the Rabbit around, using the head to trace my lips. That was a little easier to take, but I wanted to come so badly.

"Please, Nick, please!"

"Not yet." He pulled the egg out of me by its cord and stopped what he was doing for a minute while I lay back and rested. Then I felt the egg on my ass. He pushed it into my asshole, and I almost screamed as it stretched me. Then he shoved the Rabbit into my pussy and touched the ears to my clit. Oh my God, I definitely couldn't take anymore. I cried out as I came, long and hard, squirting, arching my back, writhing around and pushing the Rabbit out of me as Nick held it in. When I was done, Nick moved the ears back to my clit, and it almost hurt.

"Stop. Stop! That was it."

He pulled out the Rabbit and the egg and turned them off. He climbed up by my side, gave me a long kiss, and laid his head down next to mine, his body leaning on mine. We lay there, silent, for a long time.

I stroked his hair. "Whaddaya want for dinner?"

"Are we cooking or ordering?"

"I'm trying to think of what I was gonna make for dinner, and I can't even remember."

"You did enough today. Let's order something."

I laid my head on his arm. "OK."

7

Hard Stop

Melissa and I had a lunch on Thursday. Just before I left, I sent an instant message to Nick: *How you doin' today, hottie?* He answered immediately: *Missing you. What r u doing?*

Me: *On my way to lunch with Melissa.*
Nick Martone: *Damn.*
Me: *Why?*
Nick Martone: *I was gonna ask you to lunch.*
Me: *Sorry.*
Nick Martone: *Dinner?*
Me: *I thought we had a date tomorrow.*
Nick Martone: *So?*
Me: *LOL, you're so cute.*
Nick Martone: *I'm handsome.*
Me: *That too.*
Nick Martone: *I thought tomorrow was performance-based, depending on the meeting.*

Me: *It's all performance-based, stud.*
Nick Martone: *You're funny.*
Me: *Yes, I am.*
Nick Martone: *So Friday?*
Me: *Yes, Friday.*
Nick Martone: *We're going out.*
Me: *Where?*
Nick Martone: *Let me worry about that. I'll pick you up at 7.*
Me: *OK, ttyl.*
Nick Martone: *OK, cutie. Bon appetite. I guess I'll get a sandwich or something.*
Me: *I hear Hoagies has a $4 special.*

I left for the restaurant. I was the first one there. I sat down and admired the bright-color accents—curtains, pillows, tablecloths—all over the room. The place always felt so festive, but the sitar music had a calming effect, so the net result was unspecified happiness.

Melissa came in and sat across from me. "So, is Nick Martone still coming around?"

He wasn't a tomcat, despite his reputation. "Yes."

The busboy poured her water. "That's a long hookup."

"It's not just a hookup. We're together."

"Together-together?"

"Yeah."

She got the pity eyes. "Oh, honey, what did he tell you?"

"It's not like that. We like each other."

Her eyes narrowed. "And you know this how?"

"He told me he liked me." I heard myself sounding pouty.

"I bet he says that to all the girls."

"No, it's not like that. He brought it up, and it was this whole discussion about why I was holding back on him when he'd given me every indication that he liked me. He was mad that I wasn't getting it. He said flat out that he liked me and that he wanted us to be dating, not just hooking up."

"Really? Huh."

The waiter came and told us we could go up to the buffet. Melissa went first, and I stayed with our stuff.

Once I went and came back, she said, "So he went out of his way to tell you he liked you? Weird."

"Thanks."

"No, I mean...you know what I mean. He's a player. He's always been a player. And now he's not a player?"

"I get that you worry about me, but I don't think you have to. He was very sincere. It was like he was desperate to convince me. And it's not like I was cutting him off or anything. We were still sleeping together. The only motivation he had, as far as I could tell, was that he has feelings for me. And he shows me all the time. He's really sweet."

Melissa looked dubious. "How does he show you?"

"He holds my hand; he brings me flowers; he always wants to stay the night; he told me his mother would like me."

Her eyebrows shot up. "His *mother*? OK, maybe he does mean it."

"I believe him. I really do."

She sighed. "I hope he is sincere, for your sake."

"I'm a big girl. Speaking of which, what's going on with the wedding?"

"Oh my God, I mentioned bridesmaids in front of Megan, and she automatically assumed she was in the wedding party."

I laughed and quickly slapped my hand over my mouth. "I'm sorry; it's not funny, but it is funny."

"No, it's not. What am I gonna do?"

"Tell her no."

"Oh my God, how the hell do I do that?"

"I don't know. Maybe say you've got a bridesmaid budget and your mom insists on including your cousin?"

"That's good; I'll try that."

We talked dresses and flowers and decorations, talked shop for a while so we could expense the meal, and when we left, Melissa hugged me. "Be careful, OK?"

"I will."

When I got back, I worked on my assignment for the next Alliance meeting. Fortunately Melissa did remember what I was supposed to do, so I didn't have to call Jennifer. I had to write a letter to several members of Congress asking to extend tax credits for sustainable energy. Boilerplate. I wrote it and didn't have to think.

I was proofing it when Nick called. "Hey, Angie."

"Hey."

"Bad news. I can't do Friday night."

What? "Crap."

"I know. I've got to take this guy to dinner. He could be a major donor, and Friday's his only availability."

"That's OK."

"No, it's not. I wanna see you. Plus we have the meeting tomorrow. How about Saturday night?"

"I can't. I'm working an event with my club that day, and I'll be exhausted afterward."

"Sounds interesting. What kind of event?"

It did? "The Barbecue Bash. We have a booth."

"Can I come along?"

I was completely thrown. He wanted to go to this festival, where he'd meet most of my friends and hang around the booth all day with no possibility of sex. The whole purpose of this date was supposed to be because we were all worked up from the meeting. "Are you sure? All my friends are gonna be there, and we'll be working the booth. And drinking. But mostly working. No, that's not true. It'll be about fifty-fifty."

"Yeah, I said I wanna see you, and I'd love to meet your friends."

"OK. Sure. I can pick you up. It's early, though. We have to be there at eight. Is seven thirty OK?"

"Seven thirty's fine. I'm looking forward to it." I heard a muffled "Be right there, Dave," and then he said, "Shoot, they need me. I gotta go. I'll see you at the meeting tomorrow."

"OK, yeah, see you then. Bye."

"Bye, hottie."

Huh. He wanted to meet my friends—about twenty of them all at once—but he'd have no trouble, as socially gifted as he was. I hoped we wouldn't see anyone from work, but if we did, who was to say Nick and I didn't run into each other there too? We could pull it off.

On Friday morning, dressing for the meeting posed a problem. I wanted to look nice, but Friday was dress-down day. I picked out a pair of stretch jeans and a formfitting summer sweater. This meeting would be different. I had a plan.

The day went by surprisingly fast. I had a few meetings in the morning and a deadline looming for one of my articles. I left at one thirty for the two o'clock meeting and, thanks to Metro, got to the Hydro office with only a few minutes to spare.

Nick was already there, standing across the room with someone, folio in hand. I saw two chairs together and took the one on the right. Almost immediately, Nick excused himself from his conversation and sat down.

Jesus, Nick, could you be more obvious? Hydro Jen called the meeting to order. Old business first.

"Angie, do you have the letter you were writing?"

"I brought copies, but I sent the file to Jennifer." I turned to Wind-Power Jennifer. "You got it, right?"

"I got it. Thanks."

I slid the copies across the table. Jen started to pass them out.

Nick wrote on his pad and slid it closer to me.

You look beautiful.

I wrote on my pad.

Thanks.

He scribbled a reply.

You're driving me crazy.

I bit my lip to keep from grinning.

You ain't seen nothing yet.

It was Nick's turn to hide a smile.

Bring it, Baby!

I had to pay attention as everybody picked apart my letter. I was mark-ing changes when I felt a hand on my thigh. I glanced at Nick, and he squeezed my thigh and moved his hand to my knee. I kept writing. Slowly his hand slid up my inner thigh.

I snapped to attention as Jennifer said, "OK, so can you get those changes and send them by the end of next week?"

Nick snatched back his hand and wrote something on his pad.

I hoped nobody saw that. "Sure, no problem."

Jennifer said, "OK, next we've got mandates. Matt, can you give us an update?"

Nick was in for it now. I poured myself a glass of ice water and slipped off my shoe. My toe touched his ankle, and I took a drink. I tapped my pen on the table so that he would look over, and I showed him an ice cube between my lips. I moved it around in my mouth and reached for his leg. I rested my hand on his thigh and slowly stroked it up to his package. I lightly traced it, and I noticed he was getting hard. I gave him a final caress and moved my hand to rest on his thigh.

He wrote something down and showed me his pad.

Tease!

Yep. I was evil.

You said bring it.

He barely contained a snort.

You're mine in the elevator.

I squeezed his thigh in reply.

"On to new business," Jennifer said. "Nick, any movement on wave energy? Are they interested in joining?"

Nick snapped his head up. "I'm meeting with them next week. I'll bring it up then."

"OK, moving on," Jennifer said. "Melissa, what's going on with the expo?"

That's right, the expo. It was a few weeks away. It wasn't on my radar because one of my colleagues was working on it this year. We'd have a booth—well, everybody had a booth. It was held in one of the congressional office buildings and targeted at members and congressional staffers. Staffers mostly came for the free Ben & Jerry's and organic treats.

Our whole group was invited to a reception that night—the member companies threw it as a thank-you for all of our work. It was *the* social event of the year for us because it was the only social event of the year. Everybody got dressed up and got drunk together, and it was a lot of fun.

As we went over a few more things, I retracted my hand from Nick's thigh but not before I checked on that rising hard-on. I touched it, and he twitched, obviously trying to control himself. If it wasn't wood before, it was definitely wood now.

Just before the meeting ended, Nick wrote me another note:

Elevator!

I nodded, but Melissa motioned for me to come with her. She ushered me into the ladies' room. We chatted with the women in there, pretending to wait for stalls. When they left, Melissa said, "Do you come to these just to flirt now?"

"Pretty much." I shrugged. "Were we that obvious?"

She shook her head. "No, not that bad, but I knew what was going on."

"Do you think anybody else noticed?"

She gave a dismissive wave. "I doubt it. They were all into the meeting."

"Whew. Good." I let out a breath I hadn't realized I was holding.

"So are you two gonna get a room now?"

"If Nick had his way, we would."

She checked her hair in the mirror. "I was kidding."

"Yeah, he's not."

She laughed and turned to look at me. "Damn, girl! So what are you gonna do?"

"Fool around in the elevator."

She sighed. "Man, I miss being single."

"No, you don't. You just think you do."

Her eyes got starry. "Yeah, Jason's pretty great." She really did love him.

"Yes, he is."

She snapped out of it. "Oh, I guess I should leave before you, huh? So the elevator's free?"

"Yeah, we're waiting until everybody's gone."

"OK, then. I'll see ya later." She winked. "Have fun!"

I smiled. "We will." I let her go, put on some lipstick, and waited until I heard the elevator door close. I headed toward the reception room. I heard a flush and Nick walked around the corner. He must've flushed for effect. His eyes had the seriousness and determination that I recognized from the bedroom.

He attempted nonchalance. "Are you working the expo?"

"Yep, I'm a booth bunny."

He winked. "I'll stop by."

The elevator dinged. My body strained to touch him. We got on, and the minute the door closed, he grabbed and kissed me, smashing my lips.

I pulled away and reached for that raging hard-on. "Today's your day," I said as I unbuttoned and unzipped his pants. I slid my hand inside his underwear and freed him, pulling hard. He leaned his head back, and his breath caught in his throat. With the other hand, I pointed to the elevator buttons. I whispered in his ear, "See if we can stop this thing."

Obediently, he searched the panel for a switch, found one, and flipped it. It was an old building, and we steeled ourselves, but no alarm sounded as a result. I put my notebook on the floor, kept my grip on Nick as I kneeled on it, and put my mouth around him. He let out a high-pitched moan, and I thought he might just collapse. I kept going. I pulled him and sucked him and loved hearing him moan. I'd barely gotten into rhythm, when he cried out and shot into my mouth. I hate to swallow, but I did it for him—payback for the last elevator encounter and all those blow jobs he wouldn't let me give. It's not like I could spit cum onto the elevator floor anyway. He was still breathing hard as I let him go.

He grabbed my arms and pulled me up. "C'mere." He hugged me against him and tried to catch his breath. "That was fantastic. Thank you."

"I'm glad you liked it," I said, leaning my head on his chest. He lifted my chin and kissed me.

The elevator's alarm kicked in—we must've been stopped too long. I giggled.

"Lemme get dressed."

I gave him space as he tucked himself back into his briefs and zipped himself up. I flipped the switch, and the elevator started to descend. He pulled me close and kissed me, our lazy tongues playing. The elevator dinged, and we parted. I picked up my notebook just before the door opened. We made our way through the small crowd waiting for the elevator. We knew we caused the backup.

As soon as we got outside, we laughed and laughed. We tried to recover, but every time we looked at each other, we'd start again. He grabbed my hand and held it as we walked to the Metro. I scanned the street, looking for colleagues. At the station, he took me in his arms and kissed me. And kissed me, like we were starting all over again. I wanted the kiss so much that I put aside my fears of being seen and melted in his arms.

He pulled away. "I guess I should let you go."

"No." I kissed him again, for a long time, until the kiss broke naturally.

He held my hands. "So Saturday morning?"

"Yeah, Saturday morning. Seven thirty."

"See ya then." He gave me a quick kiss, and I headed for the escalator. I stopped at the entrance and stood aside as I watched him walk away. I wished we could just ditch work and play together. I felt light and happy and couldn't wait to see him again.

8

Live Demo

I headed out bright and early Saturday morning, picked up two dozen New York bagels and some cream cheese, and made it to Nick's building in less than ten minutes. I called him, and he came down.

He opened my little green Honda's door and said, "Good morning," as he slid into the worn tan seat beside me. He leaned over for a kiss.

I obliged. "How was your donor dinner?"

"Would've been better if I didn't have to cancel on you, but other than that, it went well. I'm ninety percent sure I convinced him to donate. He's in our target demographic."

"Well, I missed you last night, but at least it was worthwhile."

"I missed you too." He took my free hand. "Sooo...what do we do at the Barbecue Bash?"

"We hang out under the tent, collect money for charity, get drunk, and recruit members."

"Sounds like fun. What's your target demographic?"

"People who want to join our group."

"So you're not picky."

"Nope, the more the merrier. The more people we have, the more ideas we generate, the more money we raise for charity."

"What kinds of charities?"

"Lots of different ones—Alzheimer's, the Heart Association, Chesapeake Bay Preservation, food banks."

"Wow, you guys really do a lot."

"Yep, that's what we're here for."

"What did you do last night?"

"Went to happy hour. One of my friends hosts a happy hour every Friday."

"Where?"

"Different places. Last night's was at the Capitol Brewpub."

"Ooho, I love their pretzels."

"Me too. I found out how to make the dipping sauce too."

"You'll have to show me."

"Sure, sweetie." I squeezed his hand.

We got to the event and were directed to parking in a small garage under a low-rise office building. I grabbed the bagels on the way out of the car. "I gotta get the cooler out of the trunk."

Nick rushed to the back of the car. "I'll get it."

I pressed the button, and the trunk popped open, revealing my big blue cooler, with cup holders, on wheels.

Nick picked it up, strained, and grunted, "What's in it?"

"Beer and food. Mostly beer."

He wrangled it to the ground. "Anything else?"

"No, we're ready."

Nick took the handle, and the gravelly sound of the wheels on pavement accompanied us as he pulled the cooler behind him. As we walked toward the park, we got the lay of the land. The festival was in a big clearing, surrounded by old leafy and evergreen trees, next to the Potomac. We got to the paved walk and followed it until we found the club's tent—tents. They had three pop-up tents, which were all lined up next to the club's huge pirate-ship display.

"Hey, guys. Good spot," I said.

Christopher, our stocky club president, said, "Yeah, everybody'll pass us coming in." He raised one eyebrow. "You brought some help?"

"Yeah, this is my friend Nick," I said.

Nick held out his hand. "How do you do?"

Charmer. I've always wanted to say that when I meet someone, but I never remember.

"Good to meet you, Nick. Any friend of Angie's is a friend of ours." They shook hands. "You can park your cooler over there." He gestured vaguely.

We started toward the back of the tent, but Nick stopped and whispered in my ear, "I'm your *friend*?"

"Yes?"

He frowned. "We're more than friends."

I whispered, "So I'm supposed to say 'This is Nick. We're more than friends'?"

"You could introduce me as your boyfriend."

What? "I could?"

"Well, I can't be your boyfriend at work. Can I at least be your boyfriend here?"

How weird was it that a guy would push for that? "Really? I mean, that's a step past where we are."

He raised his eyebrows. "Is it?"

"We've only been seeing each other a few weeks."

"So?"

"And that would mean we're exclusive." I squinted at him, trying to read his reaction.

"Are you seeing anybody else?"

I shrugged. "No."

"Neither am I. Do you want to see other people?"

Um, say it? Don't say it? "No."

"Neither do I. And here we are."

I blinked. "I guess so."

"Try to reign in that enthusiasm, Angie."

"No, it's just that you surprised me with all this. Sure, then I guess that's it."

"Then it's done. Now please introduce me as your boyfriend."

"OK."

"Kiss?"

I kissed him. Boyfriend? And Melissa didn't think he was serious. There were already about fifteen Hawaiian shirt–clad people under the tents, and I introduced Nick as my boyfriend. Trying on the word felt weird but good. It had been a long time since I'd had a real boyfriend.

Nick went to help lift some equipment, and my brainy blond girl-friend took me aside. Wide-eyed, Jamie said, "He's cute—really cute. Tell me about him. Where'd you meet him?"

"He's a work acquaintance. We met at a conference."

"Nice. What's he do?"

"He runs an environmental fund."

She raised her eyebrows. "Runs it, huh?"

"Yep."

"Sooo," she said, her voice singsongy, "how long have you been dating?"

"Only a few weeks." I was still getting used to it myself.

"And it's serious already. Wow."

"Well, we just had that discussion five minutes ago, and he said he preferred the term 'boyfriend.' He was upset that I told Chris that he was my friend."

"That's such a girl thing."

"Right? I know."

She smiled. "Well, I think you make a cute couple."

"Thank you."

We worked to get the booth set up, and Chris explained our fund-raising. "We're selling leis for a dollar apiece. We need a couple of people out front hawking leis and putting leis on people—kissing is optional—and two people taking money. You know the drill. And we have the membership table right here. We need two people to man the table."

"I'll hawk leis, Chris," I said. "Nick will help."

We headed toward the giant blue storage bin of leis under one of the folding tables. Together we took them out and put them on top of the table.

I briefed Nick. "So when people start coming in, our line is usually 'Get lei'd for a dollar,' with variations depending on how drunk we get."

"Got it." He said into my ear, "Do you wanna get laid for free?"

I smiled. "Mmmm, that sounds nice. Tonight?"

He winked. "Maybe tonight. Maybe not."

Just then the Millers, a boomer couple who'd been in the club forever, came up to the table and started to set up their cashboxes. We talked procedure for a bit, and then people began to wander into the park.

I swung a lei above my head. "Get lei'd for charity! Get lei'd for a dollar!"

A middle-aged woman came up to me. "I wanna get lei'd."

"OK, pay over there, and the gentleman will lei you." I handed the lei to Nick. He lei'd the women; I lei'd the men. After about an hour, Jamie and Chris relieved us, and we took a break.

Nick whispered in my ear, "I wanna get lei'd."

I whispered back, "One dollar."

He took my hand. "Come on." He led me into the park. We followed the paved path by several white-tented booths, heading for the woods on the other side. When we got to the tree line, he pulled me toward it. "C'mon, let's fool around."

I looked at all the people. "Are you serious?"

He leaned in conspiratorially. "You know you want to."

"You're right, I do, but won't people be able to see us?"

"Leave it to me. I'll find us a good spot." He pulled me closer and kissed me.

"Mmmm, twist my rubber arm." We kissed some more.

"Let's go." He led me into the woods.

We found a tall, leafy shrub and got behind it. Nick leaned me up against a tree and kissed me hard. I melted into him. He slid his hand toward my breast. My bra top gave him easy access to it, and he pulled it up, exposing both breasts. He took one in his mouth and licked my nipple. My knees buckled, but I was leaning against the tree. He pinched my other nipple, and I arched my back, running my fingers through his hair. He let his free hand wander down to my waist, unbuttoned and unzipped my pants, and slid his finger between my lips.

I gasped. He slid a finger in and out of me and then ran it up to my clit. I stood on tiptoe and moaned as he stroked it. He moved to his knees and licked me as I felt the orgasm build. I heard a rustling several yards away and looked for its origin. The leaves were thick, but I saw a guy going to take a leak. He looked toward us; I didn't know if he could see, but I was still essentially topless. He kept looking, so he must have seen us. I watched him watch me as Nick furiously licked my clit, and I held my breath as the pleasure exploded in me. He kept going, and I felt another round of orgasm wave through me. The guy zipped up, but he kept his eyes on us.

Nick looked up. "Done?"

I was still so hot with the guy watching, but I breathed an affirmative reply. "Yeah."

"Good." He stood up, unbuttoned and unzipped, and I grabbed his dick. It felt big and hard, and it was practically pulsing. He caught his breath at my touch and pumped into my hand as he fumbled in his pocket for a condom. When he found it, he handed it to me and pulled his pants down. I ripped the package and rolled the condom onto him; he moaned. Keeping one eye on the guy in the woods, I took off one leg of my pants to give Nick better access. He pushed me up against the tree and steered into me, filling me and pumping hard. He grabbed my thighs, and I wrapped my legs around him. The tree dug into my back as he thrust into me, but I didn't want to stop. It felt so good to have him in me and so focused on us.

He pushed harder and faster, and I exhaled with every pulse. I knew how that turned him on. It worked, because he strained, practically growling, and screwed his face up as he shot into me. He jerked and jerked, and he leaned against me when he was done, breathing hard. I released my legs and held him to me. I didn't want to let go.

He breathed into my ear, "Oh man, that was so hot!"

I said, "Where's my dollar?"

Still breathing hard, he replied, "That lay was worth more than a dollar."

"Damn right it was." I let go of him for a second to fix my bra top.

"Aww, don't cover 'em up, gorgeous!"

I smiled. "Well, so far you and the guy in the woods are the only ones who've seen them. I'd like to keep it that way."

He pulled up his pants. "What guy in the woods?"

"This guy took a leak right over there, and he watched us."

"And you didn't tell me?"

I put my pants back on. "You were busy, and I didn't want you to stop. Plus it made me really hot."

He shook his head. "You are so sexy, Angie Pappas."

"Takes one to know one."

He took my hand and led me out of the woods. "Next time we get caught, let me in on the secret. I want to enjoy it too."

"OK," I said. "Next time. I didn't know how you'd react."

"Of course, now I've gotta think about some guy who saw my girl-friend's ta-tas."

"I've been your girlfriend for an hour. Now you're all possessive?"

"Yes, I am possessive of your tits. They endlessly amuse me, and I'd like to have them to myself."

I giggled. "You did."

"Seriously, though, when something that hot happens, tell me."

"OK."

We got to the edge of the woods. He stopped to hug and kiss me for a while. "Mmmm, I like having a girlfriend."

I rested my head on his shoulder. "I like being one."

"Wanna take a look around?"

We wandered around the festival, stopping to taste pulled pork, chicken, brisket, and dip pretzel sticks in fifteen kinds of barbecue sauce. We bought some venison jerky from the jerky guy, tasted six dif-ferent kinds of mustard from the mustard guy, and got some free lizard stuff from the insurance booth. Then we checked out the blues band for a little while—I loved leaning back against him at the edge of the crowd.

On our way back to the club's tent, I noticed a familiar face. There was Sharon Burke, in her Birkenstocks, checking out some art at one of the tents.

I nudged Nick. "Shit! Sharon Burke, at eleven o'clock. You go that way; I'll go around."

"You don't have to do this, Angie."

"Yes, I do. Now go!"

Nick shook his head, but he obeyed. Sharon was heading toward me.

I waved as she approached. "Hi, Sharon."

"Hi, Angie, are you enjoying the Bash?"

"Yeah, I'm volunteering, raising money for the Alzheimer's Association."

"Oh, that's nice. Have you been here long?"

"I've been here since this morning."

"I was thinking of going to see Flatfoot Murphy. Have you caught him at all?"

"I haven't gone over there, but Skids Monroe was good," I said.

"Hmm, I'm going to check out some of the art tents. I love the samples they give here too. I just had some jerky and some mustard. I bought some of the mustard. It's really good. You should try it. My girlfriend's over there. Looks like she's calling me. I'll see you later."

Thank God. I didn't want to be stuck talking to her for half an hour. I headed straight back to the club tent and sat down on a cooler, next to Nick, who was drinking beer and chatting with my friends. I loved that he could hold his own with twenty people he'd just met.

Chris came over and asked us if we'd hawk leis again. "Our sales dropped off after you left. Can you get 'em goin' again?"

I said, "Sure, and now we've got more beer in us. This should be fun."

We grabbed some leis and relieved the current team. Nick started. "Get lei'd for charity! Get lei'd for a dollar!"

I'd had enough beer to kick it up a notch. "Sure, I'll respect you in the morning! Get lei'd for a dollar!"

Nick got into the spirit. "Nothing like a cheap lei! Get lei'd for a dollar!"

"Need to get lei'd? One dollar!"

We got some customers—a couple. I lei'd him, and Nick lei'd her. We kept drinking and hawking for another couple of hours, until we ran out of leis. The club kept the membership table up, but Chris said we could go if we wanted to.

On the way back to the car, Nick said, "That was fun, Angie. Thanks for taking me and introducing me to your friends."

"I'm glad you liked it. It was a lot of fun with you." I gave him a kiss.

He looked concerned. "You know we didn't have to run away when we saw Sharon."

"Um, yes, we did," I said.

He shook his head. "No, Angie, we didn't. I really would have liked to come out of the relationship closet."

"I can't do that, Nick. I've got a lot to lose."

He let out a loud sigh. "No, you don't. It's *your* personal life."

"How many times do we have to go over this? When your reputation affects mine, I suffer professionally."

He shook his head. "So you're ashamed of me?"

"No, no, I'm not. I'm really proud, in fact, but I can't look like I fell for this player who may have a financial influence over my company."

He looked mad. "Whereas I'm happy to be with you, and I want everybody to know it."

I stepped closer and locked eyes with him. "I really wish you would respect me on this."

"I do respect you. I just respectfully disagree."

We got to the car. I popped the trunk, and he put the cooler in for me. He opened his door and sat down, silent.

I got in, started the car, and made my way out of the parking lot. Nick still wasn't saying anything. We drove up the GW parkway, still in silence.

I couldn't take it anymore. "Nick, I'm sorry, but I have to keep us quiet. For a while."

He pouted. "How long is a while? You're a writer, Angie; give me a deadline."

"Until we know whether it's gonna work."

"It is working."

God, men were so absolute. "It hasn't been long enough to tell. And what about you? How long are you going to be able to stay with one woman?"

"Are you saying you don't trust me?"

"No. I trust you. I just wonder how long I'm gonna keep you amused." That was it, wasn't it?

"Amused? You keep me more than amused, Angie. I love being with you, and it sucks that you can't believe that."

"It's not that I don't believe it. I love being with you, too, but I ask myself, how long is this guy—this guy who's been essentially a player for as long as I can remember—how long is he going to stay interested in one woman?"

He shook his head. "It's not about how many women for me. It's about the right woman."

I didn't know what to say to that. "We'll talk about it, OK? One more month, and if it's working, we'll out ourselves. How about that?"

"Well, I wanted you to be my date at the expo reception. But that's too early for you." He scowled.

"Please, Nick. I just want to be sure."

His expression was still dour. "We'll talk about it."

"Do you want me to drop you off?"

"Yeah. I'm leaving for Mass tomorrow, so I won't see you this week."

Oh God, the timing couldn't be worse. "OK, well, I'll see you when you get back." Right?

"Yeah, sure." He got out of the car. "See you then." He closed the door and walked toward his building.

No kiss? Was he that pissed? And he'd be pissed for a week. Fabulous.

As I drove home, I couldn't stop thinking. Was this it? Was it over? If he intended to see me again, wouldn't he have said something like "I'll call you from the road" or "I'll e-mail" or something equally comforting? And, oh my God, this was the first time he'd ever left me without making plans for our next date.

But what could I have done? He knew the deal. He knew that I had to keep us quiet. Maybe he was pissed that I kept putting all the blame for it on him, but it was what it was. He was the player; I was not. And it *was* his reputation that would hurt mine. What was I supposed to do about that? Make something up to spare his feelings? Good relationships were built on honesty, right? I was just being honest.

By the time I got back to my apartment, I felt like my head would explode. Fortunately, I was exhausted, and all I had the energy for was TV. I found a show that took my mind off Nick a little and drifted off. I woke up at nine o'clock, took some ibuprofen, brushed my teeth, and went to bed. As I lay in bed, I felt an emptiness in my gut. Had I lost the best thing I ever had? Oh my God, he *was* the best thing I ever had, wasn't he? Dammit, I wouldn't let myself believe that until now. And now he could be gone. Shit.

9

Self-Evaluation

Sunday was a long, dreary blur of tears, stress eating and shuffling around my apartment. I'd lost him. I knew it. Somehow I made it to Monday, when I could focus on something other than Nick. I raided my active file for everything that would require complete concentration. I went to the gym and tried to read on the bike, but thoughts of Nick kept creeping into my head. What had I done? Was it salvageable? What could I do to fix it? One minute we were fine, the next done. And now he was traveling, and he'd pick up some woman in the hotel bar and sleep with her. I knew it.

Thankful to be back at work in the afternoon, I laser-focused on projects, even worked late, because I didn't want to leave and have to think about Nick. I left the office at seven, hopped on the Metro, and headed home. I tried to focus on my book and, still in laser mode, succeeded for the most part.

At home, I took out some leftover salad and bread. It was tough to eat, because my throat was tight, and the empty feeling in my gut made swallowing hurt. I wished I were one of those people who couldn't eat when they were upset, but the ice cream could attest that I was not that lucky. Just sitting there and focusing on losing Nick, tears started to flow. I let them slide down my cheeks and into my salad bowl.

My computer dinged with an e-mail. Grateful for something else to focus on, I crossed the room to get it. I opened it.

Nick Martone: *Are you OK?*

Oh my God, Nick! Wow, that was a really weird timing. Why was he asking if I was OK? I scrolled down.

Nick Martone (5:32 p.m.): *Hey, sorry I haven't touched base sooner. I was flying yesterday, and they kept me busy all day today. I'm just now heading to the hotel. I miss you. What's going on with you? Give me a call tonight.*

The time stamp said 5:32 p.m.? Two hours ago? Where the hell was I? He must've sent it while I was away from my desk. Dammit, why didn't I check my e-mail before I left? Or my Blackberry on the Metro?

My shoulders relaxed. It wasn't over! I made myself crazy for nothing. My throat was still tight, so I took some deep breaths before I called.

He answered right away. "Hi, cutie."

What a relief to hear his voice! "Hi."

"I miss you."

I exhaled. "I miss you too."

"How come you didn't answer my e-mail? I was worried."

Oh my God, Angie, you are such a drama queen. "I just saw it. I was worried too."

"About what?"

I took a deep breath. "I thought we broke up."

"What? Why would we break up?"

"Well, you left the car mad on Saturday. You didn't kiss me. You didn't invite me up, and then I didn't hear from you."

"Angie. Please. Just because we have a fight does not mean we break up. I didn't invite you up because I was really tired—you were right, the Barbecue Bash was exhausting. And then yesterday I was traveling; the plane was overbooked, and they lost my car reservation—everything became a huge clusterfuck, so I didn't have time to get in touch. But I was thinking about you. And today they kept me busy all day. But you're right about the kiss. I was mad about avoiding Sharon."

Well, at least I got one thing right. "Oh."

"So why didn't *you* get in touch? Is that exclusively my job? I would hope that this relationship goes both ways. If you thought we were in such a bad state, why didn't you at least ask me?"

Yeah, Angie, why? "I figured that we broke up, and you didn't want to hear from me."

"Angie, please talk to me before you jump to conclusions. I was mad in the car Saturday, but I wasn't 'over you' mad. And if I was mad and wanted to break up with you, I'd have said so. You absolutely would have known. Did you really think I'd walk away just like that?"

It all seemed so stupid now. "I didn't know."

"I hope you don't think I'm that guy. But I'm sorry we had a misunderstanding. So we're clear, we're still together. So, what's going on this week?"

"I'm sorry too. Nothing much going on. I have a happy hour Wednesday, but other than that, it's quiet."

"Do you have a free night this weekend? I want to take you to a nice dinner."

I knew better than to object to dining in public. "OK."

"And don't worry, we'll go someplace our people can't afford."

Ah, fancy dinner with Nick sounded nice. "I could do either night."

"Let's do Friday. I want to see you as soon as possible."

Hearing that made me feel better than I had in days. "OK, Friday."

"Let's get dressed up too, OK?"

"Ooo, I love dressing up."

"Good. So I'll make reservations, and I'll pick you up at seven."

I smiled. "OK."

"I'll call you tomorrow, but please e-mail me during the day. I miss you."

I was so happy to say it. "I miss you too."

"Talk to you tomorrow."

My shoulders relaxed. "OK, good night."

"Good night, cutie."

It felt so good to talk to him, and I was so relieved that I couldn't stop smiling.

Somehow I made it through the rest of the week—Nick and I e-mailed several times a day and talked almost every night.

Nick got back to town Friday morning. He e-mailed me when he touched down.

Can't wait to see you tonight. I'll pick you up at your place.

I e-mailed back: *Me either. (Neither?) I'll see you then.*

I felt almost giddy about our date. I went straight home after work to change. I picked out my red cocktail dress with the plunging neckline and just enough forgiveness in the hips to camouflage my saddlebags. I picked my red, fuck-me pumps to go with it. I dried my hair with a diffuser to get more curls and did my makeup—plenty of mascara and bright red lipstick. I spritzed some perfume, and I was ready.

Nick showed up right on time, and I buzzed him in. When I opened the door, he was holding a huge bouquet of multicolored roses. "Happy anniversary," he said with a big smile.

"What? Um, thank you." I took the flowers. "What anniversary?"

He smiled, smug. "As of yesterday, we've been together one month."

"We have?"

"Yes. God, I thought women were all into counting this stuff."

"Usually we are. But I wasn't looking at the calendar."

He kissed me. "Well, happy anniversary anyway, gorgeous." He hugged me and wouldn't let go. "I missed you."

"I missed you too. You're awesome, you know that?" He really was.

"You're not so bad yourself." He smiled and put his hands on my waist. "You look fabulous."

I kissed him. "So do you." He was wearing a navy blue suit, white shirt, and a yellow tie with blue anchors on it.

He took my hand. "Are you ready to go?"

"I'm ready. Where are we going?"

He smiled. "Eighteen hundred."

"Ooo, fancy!"

"I wanted to celebrate. Plus, we had to go someplace out of our esteemed colleagues' price range."

We left my apartment and walked to the car, holding hands. He drove a red Thunderbird convertible.

"Very nice," I said as he opened my door.

"Thank you. I figured, why wait for my midlife crisis to drive a hot car?"

"It's sexy." Did I expect any less?

He winked. "Is it?"

We drove through Arlington and crossed Key Bridge into Georgetown, holding hands on the center console. We valet parked the car, and Nick ushered me into the restaurant. We had a very nice table by the window, and Nick ordered real French champagne. The place was in a historic colonial building, lots of decorative trim with hunt prints, white tablecloths, and votive candles in old-fashioned mini lanterns. It was my first time there. The restaurant was well known, but very expensive, so regular people dined there only on very special occasions.

We held hands across the table until we got our drinks, acting all moony. When our champagne came, Nick raised his glass. "To one month."

"To one month." We clinked.

"And you were worried it wouldn't last this long."

It was only a month, but it was probably his longest relationship ever. Otherwise why did he think it was such an accomplishment?

"The wind guys and I showed me some really pretty lighthouses on the Cape. I'd love to show them to you. Very nice romantic spots. We should go up this summer."

A trip. Wow, we had some serious momentum. "That would be really nice."

"They had some beautiful rocky beaches there, too, but the water's really cold."

"I went there when I was a kid. I love to watch the waves on the rocks."

His eyes sparkled. "Then we should go. See about taking some time off in August."

Oh, so he was projecting that we'd be together two more months at least. Damn, he *was* serious. And it felt good. Comforting. I really missed him this week, and I didn't want to be separated again.

He turned his attention past me, smiled, and stood up. My boss stood next to our table, smiling like Santa Claus. He looked good, his considerable girth in a black-fitted suit. He'd even trimmed his salt-and-pepper beard. Shit! Busted. There was nowhere to go.

Nick offered his hand. "Hi, Al, good to see you. How've you been?"

"Good, good." Al looked surprised to see me. "Hi, Angie, you look fantastic."

I sputtered. "Thank you. I didn't know you liked this place."

Ever poised, Al said, "I do, but I don't come very often. It's a bit pricey. Hmm, maybe I'm paying you too much." He winked.

I laughed. "No danger there."

"Well, I don't want to take up too much of your time. I just wanted to say hello. Good seeing you, Nick."

They shook hands. "You too, Al. We'll have to have lunch sometime."

"I'd like that." He went back to his table, where he pointed us out, and his wife and I shared a wave.

Once he was gone, I groaned, "Oh, my fucking God. I can't believe—of all the people to run into!"

Nick was perfectly calm. "He wasn't upset, Angie."

Oh God, oh God! "Yeah, we'll see what he has to say on Monday. I may be needing a job."

"Oh please, Al would never fire you for dating me. He's not that kind of a guy."

"No, you're right. He's not. But what *would* he do?" I tried not to freak out, failed.

Nick took my hand. "Don't worry until there's something to worry about."

I tried to keep my voice even. "Easy for you to say."

"Don't let it ruin tonight. Honestly, Angie, it's not the end of the world. Even if you did lose your job, someone would snatch you up in a minute. You're very good at what you do."

"Yeah, but..." Oops, I knew better than to go there. I took a deep breath. "OK. I'll deal with it Monday."

"Thank you. Hey, are you busy next weekend?"

I welcomed the change of subject. "Not really; why?"

"I missed you. I wanna see you again."

How sweet of him. "OK. Do you wanna go out to the wineries?" I'd been wanting to go for a while.

"Definitely," he said. "That would be fun."

The worry crept back in. "I'll need to get drunk after facing Al on Monday."

"Stop. He's a decent guy. You'll be fine."

The chateaubriand for two was scrumptious, and Nick remained in romance mode during the whole meal. When we left the restaurant and were waiting for the valet, he said, "So where are we going?"

"My place?" I'd cleaned up last night.

"OK. I can't wait to touch you."

I turned, put my arms around him, and kissed him. "Me neither."

When we got back to my apartment, we locked up, and kissed, and kissed, and kissed. I untied his tie and started to unbutton his shirt. He reached around me and unzipped my dress. "Bedroom," he breathed. We made our way there. I turned toward him, and he pushed my dress off my shoulders, letting it drop. He held me at arm's length. "I missed your body."

I hugged him inside his shirt. "I missed yours." I kissed him, lifted the shirt off him, and helped him out of his T-shirt. I stroked his chest. God, I missed it!

He reached behind me, unhooked my bra, and let it drop. He took my breasts in his hands, held them, and then he slid his hands down to my panty hose.

"I'll get those," I said. I tried my best, but there is no sexy way to remove control-top panty hose. I struggled one leg out while the other bound my thigh and then pulled off the other leg, hopping on one foot.

We both laughed. Nick reached down and squeezed my ass while I undid his belt and pants. I got them off, and he pulled me to him and kissed me. He broke our kiss and steered me to the bed. He climbed up to it and sat behind me, straddling me and facing the 1970s mirrored closet doors.

"Look at you," he said. "You're so beautiful." He moved his hands up my torso to my breasts, holding them for a second before he touched the nipples. He whispered, "Watch."

I felt a tingle from my nipples to my crotch. Watching him play with my nipples made me want to climb up on his dick.

He hooked a finger inside my panties. "Take this off."

Reluctant to move from his touch, I stood up and took my panties off.

"Sit," he said, scooting backward. "Back here."

I shifted back on the bed until I was leaning on him again. He started on my nipples again. He whispered, "Show me your pussy."

I pulled my knees up and spread my legs wide open. I could see his eyes on my pussy in the mirror as he pinched my nipples. I spread wider, inviting his touch. "It's beautiful," he said, still playing with my nipples.

I couldn't take it anymore. "Touch it. Please."

He slid one hand down to it. I watched his fingers stroking my lips and then watched one disappear into me. I gasped. He slid his finger in and out, in and all the way out, and caressed my lips some more, teasing. My pussy swelled with sensitivity. He moved his hand up toward my clit, stroking around and around it as I tried to steer him to it. "Not yet," he said and kept rubbing, teasing. "Keep watching."

That was easy. I couldn't take my eyes off the mirror, and I felt the orgasm building. Something about him still wearing briefs and me being completely naked heightened the heat. He kept playing with my lips until electricity shot through me, and I came, pushing my pussy into his hand and breathing hard.

"More?" he said.

I nodded. He dipped his finger inside me again and added a second finger. The sight of those two fingers stretching me out got the next orgasm building. He slid them in and out of me, striking my G-spot, and then took them out and trailed his fingers up to my clit. It was such a relief when he touched it. He stroked and stroked as I watched his fingers on me. I arched my back. I couldn't hold back anymore as the orgasm rocked me, and I saw myself squirt.

"More?"

"Maybe."

He moved both hands back to my breasts and played with my nipples. "Look at your pussy," he said. I watched his hands on me and my wide-open pussy, and the idea that he was watching too drove me wild. "There's another one," I whispered.

He slid his hand down to my clit, rubbing softly at first, then harder. I held my breath and willed myself to come. I was just about to take a breath when I exploded, pushing myself into his hand. When it was over, I slumped against him. He wrapped his arms around me. "Good?"

"Oh my God, Nick! Yes, good."

"Now I want to watch you give me a blow job."

"OK," I said, "lie down."

Nick shifted on the bed until he was lying parallel to the mirror. I lay down on the far side and pulled off his briefs, and he skipped a breath when I grasped and pumped his dick a few times, stroking his balls and ass with my other hand. I licked the rim around the head, playing. He moaned. I loved that he was enjoying this so much.

All at once, I took him in my mouth, and he jumped and gasped. I pumped him in and out of my mouth, still playing with his balls and ass. He arched his back and grunted. I snuck a glance at the mirror. He was watching me. I saw that my hair blocked his view and tucked it behind my ear. "Oh yeah," he said. "I wanna see you."

I kept bobbing on him, licking the head when I came up. He writhed and moaned. My jaw hurt, so I took a break, just using my hand. He looked down at me. "You're amazing."

I took him in my mouth again. He pumped himself, and my hand wandered down his ass. I found his asshole. I pushed my finger in it a little. He jumped and moaned. After a few seconds of that, he said, "Climb on top. I wanna fuck you."

I untangled myself and straddled him; then I took the condom he handed me and unrolled it on him. He moaned, "Oh!" as I guided him in. He felt so big as he thrust into me, pumping wildly. He looked at the mirror. "I love seeing you up there, watching your tits bounce." We both watched as he kept up the rhythm. "Let's flip over," he said. I climbed off him and lay on the bed. He got between my legs and lifted my feet to his shoulders. I looked at his damp pecs, his six-pack. God, he was gorgeous!

He sped up his pumping and got that look of concentration. He made his sex face and shot into me, his body jerking. When he was done, he leaned on my legs for a second. "That was so good! God, I love fucking you!"

"Me too, baby. Me too."

He extricated himself and lay down next to me. He reached out for me, and I rolled over, my head on his chest. "I missed you."

"I missed you too." I closed my eyes.

He stroked my hair and kissed my forehead. We lay there, silently content.

On Monday morning, my boss called me into his office. I sat down on the black leather love seat across from his desk, looking at the view of the alley our nonprofit office space afforded us.

Al tented his fingers. "So, when did you start seeing Nick?"

Shit, for all he'd known, that could have been our first date. What's the better answer? If I started to lie, I'd have to keep lying. "About a month ago."

"I like him." He leaned forward. "I don't know that he's the best guy to get involved with, though."

I tried to keep my voice even. "Why not?"

"Every time I've seen him out, he's with a different girl."

Oh, that. "I know."

He raised his eyebrows. "Does that mean it's a casual relationship?"

I believed it, but I hated having to say it. "No, not really. He says he's serious."

Al sighed. "I know I'm not supposed to discuss your private life, but it could affect our funding and, in turn, all of our jobs."

"I know, and I've thought about that. Believe me, I've thought about that. I know the deal. If he gives us funding, there's a question of ethics, and if he doesn't because of me, I've jeopardized our company."

Al leaned back in his chair. "That's it in a nutshell, not to mention your reputation in the business."

"Believe me, I've been over and over it in my head. That's why we kept it quiet." It felt kind of good to have someone agree with me.

Al met my eyes. "So nobody else knows?"

"Just Melissa. But Nick is pushing for everyone to know."

He looked concerned. "Interesting. Let me ask you this: Do you think it's the real deal?"

I nodded my head slowly. "I really think it is. From the very beginning, Nick's said that I was different, and he's given every indication that it's real."

"OK then, mazel tov. If a funding question comes up, we'll deal with it then. Right now we haven't applied for anything from him." He winked. "Just don't break up with him."

I smiled. "No problem there. For now."

"And just so you know, I would never fire you for anything in your personal life, but the reality is if we lose funding, we have to lose people." Al was nothing if not fair.

I looked down. "I know."

When I got back to my desk, I e-mailed Nick: *Had my talk with Al.*

Nick Martone: *What did he say?*
Me: *He said we don't have any funding issues with you right now.*

Nick Martone: *I could've told you that.*

Me: *And he told me not to break up with you.*

Nick Martone: *Smart guy. I've always liked him.*

Me: *You're so cute.*

Nick Martone: *I'm handsome. What did he say about going public?*

Me: *He said it was interesting that you want to.*

Nick Martone: *What's that supposed to mean?*

Me: *It means he knows your reputation, and he's surprised.*

Nick Martone: *Here we go again.*

Me: *You asked, and see? I'm not the only one.*

Nick Martone: *I did ask. Dammit. Are we having lunch this week?*

Me: *No.*

Nick Martone: *How about Wednesday?*

Me: *I really don't think it's a good idea, especially since I don't know what my boss thinks about going public. I'll see you Saturday.*

Nick Martone: *That's too long.*

Me: *We'll see.*

Nick Martone: *OK. Ttyl.*

Me: *OK.*

10

Working Lunch

I worked on some expo handouts Monday and Tuesday, with occasional instant messages from Nick, but truth be told, I missed him. I didn't want to wait until Saturday to see him; so when he sent me an instant message Wednesday morning, I was going to suggest a date.

> Nick Martone: *Good morning. How would you feel about lunch in private today?*
>
> Me: *Go on...*
>
> Nick Martone: *Two words: room service.*
>
> Me: *You wanna get a hotel room?*
>
> Nick Martone: *Yes, I'm dying to see you.*
>
> Me: *OK.*
>
> Nick Martone: *That was easy.*
>
> Me: *If I had a nickel for every time a guy said that...*
>
> Nick Martone: *Yeah, me too. I'll book a room and send you the details.*
>
> Me: *OK, hottie.*

Ooo, a nooner! How hot was that? I was so excited to see him that I had butterflies. Ten minutes later he sent me another instant message.

Nick Martone: *Capitol Grand Lobby, K St. 12:00.*
Me: *Can't wait.*
Nick Martone: *Neither can I, cutie. See you then!*

Lunchtime couldn't come fast enough. I tried to focus on work, but the anticipation had me bouncing off the walls. Finally, at 11:45 a.m., I couldn't take it anymore. I left the office and took the two-block walk to the hotel. It was right between our offices, so I knew Nick didn't want to waste any time either. I passed the usual homeless guy next door. He begged for money every day, and if you didn't contribute, he'd curse you out as you passed him. So if you were going to buy lunch, for example, and planned to give him your change on your way back to the office, you wouldn't, because he'd already cursed you out on the way to lunch. Marketing was not his forte.

The hotel was a concrete building with its gym-facing K Street. I'd been to the gym a few times but never to the hotel. The gym was cushy—big fluffy towels and high-end moisturizer and hair products. The lobby was bright and airy, with lots of palms in huge ceramic pots in pebbly shades of brown and wood accents. I could see my reflection in the shiny white tile floors. I sunk into a comfortable coral-colored chair and read a single-girls' magazine while I waited.

It didn't take long before I smelled his cologne and saw his black dress shoes in my periphery.

I looked up, and he smiled. He looked gorgeous in his charcoal pants, dove-gray pinstriped shirt, and black tie. "Anything interesting?"

"There's an 'I was a high-priced-hooker' article in every issue."

"At least they're not giving it away cheap. And now that they've come clean, the IRS is going to come after them for back taxes."

I stood up and kissed him. "How are you?"

He pulled me closer and started a long kiss. God, I missed his tongue! He broke the kiss and said under his breath, "That's how I am. What about you?"

I stayed close. "Me too."

"OK, let's go check in." We went to the desk, and the short Asian girl, probably fresh out of hospitality school, helped us as we paid for the room. Nick led me to the red-brown marbled elevator bank, and we waited.

"You used your real name. I thought you were supposed to use a fake name when you did this."

"That's only if you're cheating on someone."

"Oh."

The elevator came, and he gestured toward it. "After you."

When the door closed, he plastered me against the wall, and we kissed and kissed, tongues teasing. The door opened at our floor. We walked down the dimly lit hallway and found the room.

Once we were inside, we grabbed each other tight and started another long kiss. We broke, and he pulled my shirt over my head. I untied his tie and kissed him as I started to unbutton his shirt. When I was done, he unbuttoned and unzipped my pants and let them fall to the floor. I stepped out of my shoes and undid his dress pants, guiding them over his hips. He said, "I have something in mind for you."

"Oh, you do, do you?"

"I do." He grabbed his tie off the floor and led me to the bed. Gently he blindfolded me with the tie and guided me to sitting and then lying-down position. He left me, and I heard him fumble in his messenger bag; then I smelled his cologne and felt the warmth of his body back next to me. He took my hands, put them together over my head, and tied them together at the wrist.

"Oh, this is your plan?"

"Yes."

"Good plan."

I felt his hands on my cheeks. He kissed me, tongue insistent, and I felt his hands move down the front of my body to the clasp of my bra. When he unhooked it, he slipped it off, fingers grazing my nipples. He left my lips, and I felt his warmth move down my body. I felt his fingers hook onto my panties, and he took them off. He spread my legs. "Keep 'em open. I want you ready for me."

"Mmmm." I felt him move back up, hot breath on my breast, his lips around my nipple, gently sucking. He released my nipple, and I felt cool air blow, hardening it. And then I jumped as I felt his finger slide into me.

He laughed. "You like that, huh?"

"Yes."

I felt another finger go up my ass, and I arched my back. "Oh..." Then my other nipple felt a hard pinch. "Ow!"

"But did you like it?"

"Well, yes."

"Let me kiss it and make it better." I felt his warm mouth on my breast, tongue teasing my nipple. All at once he pulled his fingers out of me. He kept playing with my nipple. Then he let go, and he was gone. I jumped when his tongue touched my clit. He licked it a few times and abandoned it.

I waited several excruciating seconds for what he'd do next. Then at the same time, I felt his finger in my ass and tongue in my hole. Oh God, I could barely stand it! I writhed and moaned. Keeping his finger in me, he licked his way up my pussy, working his way back to my clit. When he touched it, I gasped involuntarily. I wished I could play with my nipples, but the ties prevented it. In answer to my wish, I felt his other hand make its way to my breast. He squeezed it and then tweaked the nipple with his finger. When he twisted it, I moaned, and that was it. I held my breath and felt the orgasm radiate.

He didn't ask if there were more. He just kept going. He moved his hand to the other breast, lifting it and rolling the nipple between his fingers. I strained, but the orgasm didn't come, so I had to catch my breath. He pushed his finger into my pussy and touched my G-spot. I arched my back and tensed, and I came, pleasure shooting outward through my body. Then he stopped. Everything. He completely abandoned me. I lay there wanting more and wondering what he'd do next.

After what seemed like hours, I felt him get on the bed between my legs. All at once I felt his dick thrust into me and out of me as he pumped. He gently slid the blindfold up, and I looked at him, realizing I'd missed watching him.

He pulled a black bandana off my hands. He looked at me and smiled; he kept pumping as he leaned down toward me and kissed me.

He pushed himself back up, and I contracted around him, letting my breath go so he'd hear every push. I reached up and played with his nipples, and he moaned. I let my hands feel the muscles in his arms and moved with him. He got that look and came, groaning and jerking on top of me. He pulled out and lay down next to me, pulling me to him.

He squeezed me. "So, you want to go get some lunch?"

"Worked up an appetite, did ya? Do we have time?"

He turned his head and looked at the clock. "We have half an hour, unless you've got more flexibility."

"I can flex a bit."

"How about the hotel restaurant? Don't worry, cutie; nobody goes there for lunch."

"Yeah, you're right. Good point; who goes to a hotel restaurant on their lunch hour? OK."

He squeezed me again and held me for a while. "We should probably go."

I sighed. "Yeah." I crawled up and kissed him. "That was awesome, hottie."

"Yeah. Yeah, it was." He smiled and then let go of me. "OK, I'm hungry."

We got dressed and headed upstairs for lunch. We had a nice, relaxed lunch and returned to the lobby. We checked out, and Nick took my hand, led me over to one of the support columns, backed me up against it, and kissed me. "Thank you for this."

"You're welcome. It was fun for me, too, you know."

"I hope so. So we're on for Saturday?"

"Yep. Saturday." He took my hand, and we headed for the door. On the street, he let go and gave me a quick kiss. "OK, I'll pick you up at what, around ten?"

"Yeah, ten's good."

He smiled. "See you then. Have fun at work."

"You too." I watched him as he walked away.

When I woke up on Saturday, it was sunny and warm—perfect for the wineries. It was a typically humid DC summer day, but the wineries were out by the mountains, so I didn't anticipate any weather problems. I showered and put on a pair of dark capri jeans and, anticipating a red-wine spill, a magenta T-shirt. I drank my coffee looking out the window and wondering how I had landed Nick Martone. If someone had told me a month ago that this would happen, I'd have laughed and laughed. Yet here we were. And to paraphrase my boss, it felt like the real thing.

Nick showed up right on time, and we headed out. He was looking hot in khaki cargo shorts and a green bowling shirt that brought out those gorgeous eyes. He held my hand on the console as we headed out on 66.

"So where do you wanna go? We need to find at least one with nice grounds. I brought a picnic lunch."

"Wow, honey, how romantic."

"I'm a romantic kind of guy."

I squeezed his hand. "And I appreciate it." I studied the wine map. "OK, so I've been to this one, and they have nice grounds with picnic tables."

"I was thinking more of you and me on a blanket."

"The grounds are nice for that too. Hmm...there are some here that I've never been to."

"I'm up for adventure."

"We should probably do all of our tasting and then eat, so we can drive home OK."

Nick moved our hands to my knee. "Good plan."

"Well, let's try some new ones, then. Oh my God, speaking of wineries, you'll appreciate this. I have a friend who goes to this winery almost every weekend in the winter. They have this lasagna lunch, and I went once—it's the driest lasagna you'll ever have. There's no sauce in the middle at all."

"Gross."

"And the thing is, she loves it! She thinks it's the greatest thing since cell phones. She invites people out all the time and raves and raves about it. It's hilarious."

"How's the wine there?"

"I have to say, the wine's good. Good dry reds."

"Maybe she goes for the wine."

"No, because she never goes in the summer when there's no lunch, and she never shuts up about the lasagna. It's hilarious."

"That's funny. A funny kind of sad. It's sad when people don't know good food. But I guess it works out for the winery."

"That it does. That it does. So I guess we'll go out toward the mountains and work our way back."

He smiled. "Just tell the GPS where you want to go, and I will follow."

I programmed the GPS and stuck it to the windshield. On the way out, we chatted about wine and food and Nick's trip to the cape while enjoying wine-country scenery that would rival anywhere in California. The green landscape was so much better than California's brown.

The first winery was gorgeous—rolling green hills, vines everywhere, and an old white farmhouse with a wraparound porch. We tried six wines, including a Viognier I loved. I bought two bottles, and we headed to the next one. Nick fell in love with a red blend there and bought several bottles. We were getting hungry, so we decided to have our picnic at the next one, but when we got there, we tasted about eight more wines first. Buzzed and happy, Nick got the picnic basket out of the car and laid our blanket out under a big tree, and we sat down.

Nick kissed me, lingered, and then sat up and opened the picnic basket. "I was thinking we'd open a bottle with lunch, but I don't think I'd be able to drive."

I smiled. "Then we'd have to find a way to pass the time until you sobered up."

"Mmmm, nice idea, but I don't see any place private here."

"So?" I laughed.

"That's right; I forgot you're an exhibitionist."

I kissed him and stayed close. "It's just that this picnic is so romantic."

"I'm glad you think so. We can get more romantic when we get home, if you're not too drunk."

"Mmmm, I'd like that, but it's not my sobriety I'd worry about. I'm not the one who has to perform."

He pulled out a loaf of bread and three hunks of cheese, peaches, and strawberries.

"Ooo, very nice, honey."

He shrugged. "It was supposed to go with wine."

"We had wine. It's perfect." I gave him a long kiss. "What kind of cheese did you get?"

"I got Havarti, Danish blue, and I found a good French Brie at Safeway."

He pulled out plastic plates and three knives. I unwrapped the cheeses and cut pieces for both of us. He broke off a piece of bread and gave it to me. I took one of the cheese knives and cut the peaches, serving some on his plate. He gave me a few strawberries and pulled two bottles of water out of the basket and handed one to me. He held it up. "Cheers."

"It's bad luck to toast with water."

"It is?"

"Yeah. I learned it on 'The West Wing.'"

"Well, we'll just toast in spirit then."

I looked into those gorgeous green eyes. "Cheers." I wanted to say "I love you," but I was just sober enough to hold back, and God, it was too soon. Wasn't it? I took a piece of Havarti and ate it with a piece of peach. I looked around the grounds. There were a lot of people picnicking—it was such a great day for it. Then I thought I recognized someone—I did recognize someone—from work. "I don't fucking believe this."

Nick looked up. "What?"

"Sophie—from ERA—is here. She's over there, with a red igloo cooler. You see her?"

"Oh yeah, that is her. Relax, Angie. It's no big deal."

"Yes, it is. She's looking for a picnic spot. I gotta go. Call me when she's gone, OK?"

"Really, Angie? You're gonna run away? Again?"

"I gotta go." I walked as casually as I could, stepping behind trees toward the tasting room. Sophie didn't see me, but I did see her wave and approach Nick. I found the bathroom and went into a stall. I sat down and tried to calm down. Sophie Black, all the way out here. Lots of people from DC went wine tasting, but come on, what were the odds? There was something like thirty wineries. And Nick sounded mad. But what was I supposed to do? He knew the deal.

My phone rang. I lowered its volume and answered.

He sounded annoyed. "Get back here!"

"Is she gone?"

Nick sighed. "No, but you don't have to hide."

"Why, did you tell her I was here?"

"No, she's nowhere near here."

I exhaled. "I can't let her see me."

Annoyed again. "Yes, you can."

"Nick, please!"

He sounded more angry than annoyed. "Forget it; I'm packing up."

Shit! "That's it? You can't wait for me?"

He growled, "I'm not playing this ridiculous game. Meet me at the car."

So now he was mad. And we had the long ride ahead of us. Great. I used the bathroom, washed my hands, and, keeping a keen eye out for Sophie, headed to Nick's car.

I got there first. I leaned against the car and waited. I spotted him trudging over the hill, carrying the basket, the blanket, and my purse. I did not like the look on his face. It was worse than after the Barbecue Bash.

Shit.

When he got to the car, he handed me my purse and opened the trunk. He put the basket and blanket in and got behind the wheel. I hoped he'd eaten enough to sober up, but what could I do? He was my only ride home. I opened my door and sat down. He backed out of the space, shifted, and hit the gas, scattering rocks in the parking lot. He raced down the drive and out to the road, all the way to the red light. He stopped and hit the wheel with both hands. "*Dammit, Angie! What the hell?*"

"Nick—"

He cut me off. "We were having a nice romantic date until *you* freaked out."

"Nick, I had to. I couldn't let Sophie see us."

"Yes, you could have, Angie. I'm sick and tired of this shit."

"I'm sorry. I've got a lot to lose."

"No, you don't. Why don't you grow up and stop worrying about what people think?"

"It's not like I'm just insecure, Nick. It's my career on the line. What if I lose my job? What happens when I look for another job? I'll be blacklisted."

"First of all, your boss is cool with us. Second, even if this was just a fling, so what? Why couldn't you get a job?"

"Well, for one thing, if we broke up and you hated me, any potential employer would be worried they'd lose funding."

"I am not that guy, and they know it."

"I don't think they do, Nick. You've never fished in the company pond before."

"Even if that was a factor, I've never been petty."

"Maybe not, Nick, but they don't know that."

"I don't think you give them enough credit."

"Maybe not, but I can't take that chance."

"That's it. That's exactly what this is about. Taking chances. The whole problem is that you don't have enough faith in me, or us, to take a chance."

"Come on, Nick, that's not true."

"Yes, it is. If you thought we had staying power, we wouldn't have to sneak around. I can't take this shit anymore. How about this? You go with me to the expo reception, as my date."

"Or what?"

"Or I can't see you anymore, Angie. My heart, my head, all the stress—I can't take it."

"So you're giving me an ultimatum."

"Take it or leave it."

"That's really not fair, Nick."

"I think it is fair, Angie. You know what's not fair? Knowing that you're so ashamed of us that you can't tell anybody. How do you think that makes me feel?"

"I told my friends in the club."

"It's not the same, Angie. It's not the same."

I took a deep breath. Exhaled. What was I supposed to do? Give up everything for him right then and there? I would've loved to go to the reception with Nick—if I wasn't risking my whole career. He didn't understand. He had total job security. I had to make a living. If I got blacklisted, what would I do? I couldn't go back to journalism. I couldn't even afford my apartment on a reporter's salary.

He just didn't get it. If I thought we were gonna get married or something, it would be a different story. But no matter how committed he seemed, I had a hard time believing he'd be able to go long term. I'd almost said I loved him. And I guess I did. But that was my fault. Dammit. I should never have let myself fall for him.

"How about after the expo? When we hit two months dating?"

"No. It's the expo or nothing."

I sat back in the seat. Why couldn't he just understand? Hold out a little longer. Just until I was sure. But honestly, what the hell was I supposed to do? My boss said if we lose funding, we'd lose jobs—no doubt starting with mine. Nick expected me to make the sacrifice for him. And what if I did? When we broke up, I wouldn't have him or a job. If I refused, at least I'd still have a job.

"I can't do that, Nick."

He spat the words and stared straight ahead. "Fine. Then I guess it's over."

My throat tightened. "I guess so." I looked out my window.

"That sucks, Angie. It really sucks. Because I'm crazy about you, and you're so fucking worried about yourself that you don't see it."

I started to feel a sinkhole open up inside me. Was he just trying to hurt me now? My voice strained. "If you were crazy about me, you'd respect me more."

"Bullshit. I respect you, Angie. But you don't respect our relationship. All the sneaking around is a load of crap."

"I respect—respected our relationship. I just have to protect myself."

"No, you don't, Angie. It's not the big deal that you think it is."

I tried to stop the tears. "What do you want me to say?"

"Say—" He interrupted himself. "I don't know, Angie. I don't know."

I didn't say anything. I looked out my window and tried to take deep breaths to keep myself from crying. I definitely didn't want him to see me cry—anymore than he already had. I stole a look at Nick. He squinted at the road, jaw set, his lips pressed together.

When we got off the highway, he drove me to my apartment and unlocked the car door. "Good-bye, Angie."

I opened my door. "Good-bye." I got out and turned away, so he wouldn't see the tears fill my eyes.

He screeched his tires, and he was gone. He was gone. The tears flowed full force as I walked up to my building and fumbled with my keys.

When I got up the stairs to my apartment, I opened the door and, once inside, threw myself on my bed and cried some more. Why? Why would he break up with me over that? Or did I break up with him? I guess I kind of did. Shit, what was I thinking?

I knew what I was thinking. I was thinking I couldn't risk my job and everything I had just for him. Him. A guy who, until me, had a different woman every night—right? How was that guy gonna be a boyfriend? At all? I mean, he seemed sincere, and I did believe him, but so did every other girl, didn't they?

But I wanted to believe it. And I did. I still did. I just didn't trust it. Shit. I hugged my pillow, shrunk into a fetal position, and sobbed some more.

I stayed in bed about two hours; then I got up and tried to decide whether to binge on alcohol or ice cream. I chose both, poured myself some Bailey's, added a shot of Jameson's, and filled a coffee mug with ice cream. I sat down on the couch, gulped my drink, and shoved ice cream into my mouth. I was alone again. I'd lost him.

He was quite possibly the best guy I'd ever had, and he was gone. I was gonna die alone. I couldn't even become a crazy cat lady because I was allergic to cats. Tears welled up and ran down my face. I tried to fill the sinkhole inside me with ice cream, but no matter how much I ate, it was still there.

I drank some more and thought about us—about that first Alliance meeting together, about our first date, about our first kiss. Thinking about the kiss made my heart hurt even more. God, if we could just go back there! If we could just start over. If we could just erase today. If I could have said "The hell with it" and greeted Sophie head-on. Then none of this would've happened. We'd be together right now—probably in bed—and everything would be OK. But it wasn't. And I had to live with that.

The alcohol was making me tired, so I curled up on the couch. I woke up about nine o'clock, and I felt OK until I remembered what happened. I didn't want to feel anymore, so I kept all the lights off and went straight to bed.

I woke up hungover on Sunday, but I welcomed the headache and nausea. It was good to feel physical pain to accompany the emotional. I sleepwalked through the day. I did manage to do some laundry, but mostly I just watched TV. It was beautiful out, but I didn't want to go outside. I didn't want to do anything. I could hardly motivate to switch out my laundry.

11

Reorganization

I was happy to go to work on Monday, to keep my mind off Nick. The first thing I did was e-mail Melissa: *Hey, I'm having a rough day. Nick and I broke up.*

Melissa answered almost immediately: *Oh shit, what happened?*

It hurt to put it into words. *We ran into Sophie out wine tasting. I hid from her, and he got pissed off. In the car he said it was over unless I went with him to the expo reception. I told him I couldn't do that.*

Melissa: *Well, is it worth losing him over?*

Tears filled my eyes as I typed my reply. *It doesn't feel like it now, but at least I still have a job.*

Melissa: *Can you do lunch today?*
Me: *Yes.*
Melissa: *Meet me at the Indian place. 12:30.*
Me: *OK.*

Melissa: *We'll talk about it.*
Me: *OK.*
Melissa: *Feel better.*
Me: *Doubt it, but thanks.*

I knew I wouldn't forget, but I didn't want anybody scheduling any meetings for me, so I put lunch on my Outlook calendar. I looked ahead at the week. Oh God, there was a preexpo meeting on Wednesday, and the expo was on Friday. Nick would be at the meeting. There was no way I could go. I clicked on the meeting time and typed in "Emergency Dentist Appointment." That would excuse me from the meeting and give me an excuse to ask a coworker to attend for me. Whew!

I sent an e-mail asking if anybody could go. A few minutes later, I had a volunteer. Good. Or not? I kind of wanted to see Nick, to see if he'd make eye contact, to see if there was any chance to get back together, to see if he was hurting too. But I couldn't face him. I just couldn't. He'd be at the expo on Friday, though. And the reception, and I couldn't skip those.

At lunchtime, I headed to the Indian place. The sunlight outside clashed with my despair. It was too bright and too hot. Melissa was inside when I got there.

At the table, she got up and hugged me. "Honey, I'm so sorry."

Choking back tears, I said, "Me too."

"It'll be OK," she said. "It just takes time." She took a sip of her water. "So you said he was mad because you hid from Sophie?"

"Yeah, and then we had a big fight, and he said if I didn't go to the reception with him, it was over." I tried to swallow, but my throat was too tight.

"So why didn't you say you'd go?"

"I couldn't. Then everybody would know. And think about it, if everybody knew, and we broke up and I got fired, I'd never get another job."

Melissa went to the buffet. When she got back, I said, "You know what the worst part is? That day, when we were at the winery, I wanted to tell him I loved him."

"Then tell him, Angie."

"No, it's too late. He's probably already hooked up with one of his 'women' by now."

"You don't know that, and even if he did, it's just revenge. Everybody does it."

"Yeah, shit, I wonder what kind of revenge he'll bring to the reception."

"You. He'll bring you. You've got to call him."

"I can't call him. I'm so humiliated. And I have to go to the reception. It'll kill me to see him with someone else."

"Oh God, Angie. Even if you do see him with someone else, you'll know she means nothing to him. You're the one he wants."

I felt sick to my stomach. "I still don't think I can handle that."

"OK, how about this? I'll find out if he's taking anyone to the reception, but you've got to call him."

"How are you gonna find out?"

"I'll talk to him at the expo meeting. Are you going?"

"No, I can't face him."

"OK, you won't be there, so it won't be weird, and I'll chat him up about the expo and the reception."

"He knows you're my friend, Melissa."

"So what? Even if he thinks you're checking up on him, maybe that's a good thing. Maybe it'll let him know you want him back."

"And how would that help? It's just more humiliating."

"No, it's not. If he knows you'll be receptive, maybe he'll make the first move and call you."

"You think so?"

"It's worth a shot."

"OK, talk to him at the meeting and tell me what he says." We had a plan. I felt a little better.

After lunch, I went back to the office. I tried to work, but I couldn't stop thinking about Nick—what he'd say, whether he hooked up with someone, whether we still had a chance. Fortunately, most of my work wasn't brain dependent. I was getting us ready for the expo—packing brochures, making sure we had all the parts for our demo fuel cell, running the slide presentation to make sure it was up-to-date, picking up our sign at the printer's. Somehow I made it through the day, and that night I tried, unsuccessfully, to distract myself with a book until bed.

With Tuesday came the agony of waiting. I knew Melissa would see Nick at the meeting on Wednesday, and I was dying to hear what he'd say. And I was scared. Scared that he'd have a date for the reception, and he'd moved on, or gone the revenge route or something equally hurtful. I had more to do for the expo—pack the candy and giveaways and make the shift schedule—but I had plenty of time to think.

I kept thinking of possible outcomes. The best possible outcome was that he'd say he didn't have a date and call me himself or give some indication that he'd like me to call. Next was that he didn't have a date, but Melissa could tell he was hurting, so I'd know he'd be receptive to a call.

Worst was that he did have a date and seemed like he was over me. And then I'd have to see him with her at the reception. That would kill me. I tossed those thoughts around all day. Somehow I made it through, and I felt some relief that I'd know something soon.

On Wednesday I woke with a mixture of hope and dread. I was dying for news—any news—from Nick. The meeting was at lunchtime, so I still had to wait out the morning. I spent most of it e-mailing Julia, catching her up on my life. I went to the gym at lunch and took a spin class to keep me from thinking. It helped because the pain in my legs afterward distracted me every time I moved.

I got back to my desk and checked my e-mail. Nothing from Melissa. No voice mails. Shit. I started to work on a slide for our presentation. I was really into it when the phone rang. I snatched the receiver.

"Angie Pappas."

"Hey, it's me," Melissa said.

Thank God! "Hey, so how'd it go?"

"Well, first of all—I never thought I'd say this about Nick Martone—but he looks like shit."

"Really?"

"Yeah, he looks like he hasn't slept in days, and he's all droopy."

"That's good, right?" I knew it was.

"Good for you, yeah."

I couldn't wait. "So did you talk to him?"

"Yeah, after the meeting I got him alone and started talking about the expo. I casually dropped the fact that he'd meet Jason at the reception, and I was able to ask who he's bringing."

"So, what'd he say?" Oh God, this was it.

"He said he hadn't thought about it."

OK. "Oh. Well, how'd he say it?"

"He tried to sound casual, but he looked sad."

"He did?" Good.

"I thought so."

"That's good then. He's missing me."

"Yeah, I think he really is. You should call him." Melissa was such a good friend.

I took a breath. "Now I've gotta think about what I'm gonna say."

"Say you're sorry and ask him to be your date at the reception."

My thoughts began to spin. "Yeah, I just gotta figure it out."

"No, just say you're sorry you were so stubborn, and you'd like to take him to the reception. In front of everybody. He'll be happy to take you back." She could get bossy.

"OK."

"Call him. Now." A good kind of bossy.

"OK." I hung up. Stared at the phone. What to say? What to say?

My boss poked his head in my office. "We're talking about the expo in the conference room."

I grabbed my pen and pad. "OK." I headed toward the conference room.

The meeting lasted all afternoon. Al was very specific on how he wanted us to conduct things in the booth. We went over schedules and giveaways, and I had to show everyone the presentation for changes. Unfortunately, there were a lot of changes, and after the meeting, I had to edit the presentation so we could have it first thing the next morning. By the time I got out of work, it was eight o'clock. I was starving and called for a pizza on the way to the Metro. The delivery guy got to my apartment a few minutes after I got there, and I wolfed down two slices. I wanted to call Nick, but I was nervous and didn't have the energy to fight it. I watched some TV to wind down and went to bed.

I woke up anxious. I always loved working the expo, but I knew I'd run into Nick, and I didn't know how it would go, if I should try to pull him aside or not, and how I'd react to seeing him in person. I dressed carefully, in stretchy black slacks and a button-down tailored shirt in cream.

When I got to work, we schlepped all the stuff down to the lobby and called for a big cab. We got to the congressional Rayburn building, and security had to inspect everything we had. It took a while, because they had a shooting about a month ago and they were extra thorough, but we got in. My boss took off to network while we set up the booth.

All the energy presenters took up a huge bare room, designed for expos like ours. We had the standard big blue fabric-covered screen, flat in the middle and concave on the ends, as a backdrop. We hung posters on either side and had a projection screen for the slides in the middle. We had a table in front of us, where we set out our brochures, handouts, and giveaways. Most of the booths looked like some version of ours, with the exception of those that didn't have a table. Most of them had a technology demonstration as their focal point, and their booth bunnies sat on stools behind it. And at the end of everything were the natural-food companies, giving out their products. I was setting up the presentation when Melissa stopped by.

Her blue eyes were wide, hopeful. "So, did you call him? You haven't said anything."

I looked at the floor. "No, I didn't call him."

"Why not?"

"It had nothing to do with him. First I had a meeting, and then I had to work late, and I was exhausted."

"Well, you'll see him here. You can talk then."

"Yeah, we can. I hope."

"Just be honest with him, Ange. Apologize. Say you want to go public."

"I'm just not sure how it'll be when we see each other."

She grabbed my shoulders to reassure me. "He's still hung up on you. It'll be fine."

I frowned. "I hope so."

"How's the booth going?" Melissa asked. "What's your giveaway?"

"Setup's going good. We have pens and stress balls."

"Oh cool, can I have some?"

"Help yourself. One stress ball, please. We don't want to run out too quickly. What's your giveaway?"

"Tote bags."

"Oh cool, that really gets your name out—everybody carrying it around. Are you at the front door?"

"We're in the first row—close enough so the bags will circulate through the room."

"Good. Can I have one?" I never knew exactly what I'd use a tote bag for, but I always wound up using them.

"Yeah, I'll bring one over. I guess I should get back."

I nodded. "OK. See you later."

"Good luck with Nick."

"Thanks."

When the booth was set and people began to trickle in, my coworkers and I took turns exploring the expo, picking up swag while it was still in good supply. When it was my turn to wander, I headed to Melissa's booth to pick up the tote bag. I wanted the bag first so that I could put all the other stuff into it.

"So, have you seen him?" she asked.

"Not yet."

Her eyes sparkled. "He's here. I saw him go by before."

"How'd he look?"

"I couldn't tell. He was too far away."

"Oh."

She leaned in. "Go get him, Angie. Go talk to him."

"I will."

I kept an eye out for Nick as I wandered the expo. I loved the mini turbine the wind people had. Hydro Jen had this little minidam with turbines that somehow sounded more like a meditation fountain than a power generator. We didn't have a technology demo. Hydrogen fuel cells' mechanisms happen at the molecular level, so there's nothing for people to see. That was why the presentation was so important to explain the process. Ethanol was giving away popcorn, because most ethanol came from corn. Ethanol was basically grain alcohol, and in ethanol plants, it was rumored they had ethanol dispensers for the employees, but as much as it would boost ethanol's popularity, they couldn't give out shots at the expo.

I got butterflies as I rounded the corner and saw Nick's booth at the end of the row. By that time, the expo was crowded, so I couldn't see who was working the booth. I gathered tchotchkes as I made my way down the row, but when I did get close enough, I saw that Nick wasn't there. I went on to the next row.

When I got back to our booth, my coworker took a break, and I fielded questions and handed out swag. I kept pretty busy. When I did have a lull, I busied myself tidying up the stuff in the booth.

"Hi."

I looked up. There he was. Nick had dark circles under his eyes, and he looked tired.

"Hi."

"You look good." He was still sweet.

"Thank you." I couldn't return the compliment. I'd be lying through my teeth.

I was about to ask to talk to him, but my coworker got back to the booth and slid behind the table. "Hi, Nick," she said.

"Hey, Ashley. How are you?"

Ashley reached into a box for more brochures. "Good. You enjoying the expo?"

"Yeah, we're having a lot of fun."

A customer walked up. I motioned for Ashley to help him. I turned back to Nick. "Hey, do you have a minute to talk?"

His eyes hardened. "Aren't you afraid people will see us together?"

"That's not fair."

He lowered his voice and leaned in. "Neither is what you did to me, Angie."

"But I—"

"I've gotta go." He turned and walked away. I thought I would cry right there, but I managed to hold it together. I told Ashley I was going to the ladies' room.

When I got there, I sat on a toilet and cried. The bathrooms were nice, with old black-and-white tile, still in good shape, but the decor clashed with the modern automatic toilets. The toilets always made me chuckle, because they squawked right before they flushed, and using congressional bathrooms always made me feel like I was taking a leak in the rainforest. The squawking didn't amuse me today, but the ladies' room was busy and noisy, so at least no one could hear me cry.

He wouldn't even talk to me. He was still mad. What was I gonna do? I didn't have a chance. And how the hell was I gonna make it through the reception? My face felt hot, and my stomach knotted. There had to be a way to get him to listen. Right? It hurt so much that I had to find a way to make it better.

But why did he say hi in the first place? Yeah, why did he? He could've walked by. I was looking down. I never would have seen him. Huh. Maybe there was still hope.

I finished crying and got up. The toilet squawked as I walked out. I splashed some cold water on my face and wished I'd brought my purse so I could fix my makeup. I got some toilet paper and wiped the mascara from my puffy eyes.

When I got back to the booth, we had tons of customers, so I fielded more questions and gave out more stuff, but I was distracted. This whole thing was about me not wanting to go public. He wouldn't let me tell him I'd changed my mind. But I had to get that message through somehow.

My boss stopped by to tell us the free Ben & Jerry's had arrived, so I went to get us some. On my way, I stopped by Melissa's booth. "Hey, you wanna go get some ice cream?"

"Yeah, sure." She turned to her coworkers. "You guys want some?" Who wouldn't? We headed over there. "So, did you talk to him?"

My throat tightened. "I tried. He came by and said hi, and I asked him to talk; he made a sarcastic comment about me not wanting us to be seen together. I said it wasn't fair, and he got mad and said what I did to him wasn't fair either."

"Ouch."

I tried to relax my throat. "Ouch is right."

Melissa considered. "But he stopped by in the first place. Did you see him first?"

"No, I was looking down. He could've walked by, and I wouldn't have even seen him."

"So he came up to you."

"Yeah."

"Huh. I'd say that's a good sign. He wanted to see you." She nodded.

"Yeah, but I fucked it up." We got to the ice-cream people. "Hey, can I get three, please? For my booth."

Melissa went next. "Can I have three? Thanks." We started to walk back. "But you still have a shot, Angie. You've got to talk to him. Pull him aside at the reception. He can't make a stink with everyone around."

"I'm gonna have to. It's my last chance."

"You have his phone number. It's not your last chance. But tonight you have the advantage of being able to look irresistible." Melissa was so smart. No wonder she was engaged.

"True. I just have to think about what I want to say."

"Just keep it simple. You're sorry. You want him back. You want to go public. That's it."

She was right, of course. "OK. I have to think about it."

"Well, this is a pretty brainless day, so you can."

I dropped Melissa off at her booth and finished my ice cream on the walk. When I got back to my booth, my coworkers took a break to eat their ice cream, and I handed out the last of the stress balls and fielded more questions. We got a few members of Congress coming to the booths. I was impressed—it's usually just staffers, and all they want is free food and swag.

I pushed my agenda whenever I could, explaining that the people who give out the money don't know the technologies. I really felt like I accomplished something by the time the expo closed. We were pretty busy, though, so I couldn't really work on a plan for the reception. My boss offered to take all the stuff back to the office, since he didn't help us work the booth, so we all got some more time to get ready for the evening.

Once I was on the Metro and I could relax and think, it came to me. I knew exactly what I'd do. When I got home, I changed into my red dress and redid my makeup and hair. Like Melissa said, I wanted to look irresistible. I wanted to, but I didn't wear my fuck-me pumps. I had to walk through Union Station, and there was nowhere I could stash sneakers at the reception, so I went with more sensible silver heels. I had to change trains to get to Union Station, but I did it on autopilot, because all I could think about was Nick. This had to work. Had to.

I hit the bathroom when I got to the station, refreshed the lipstick I'd chewed off my lips, and evaluated myself in the mirror. I looked good. Very good. Excellent! I whispered, "Here goes," and headed to the room. The reception room was on the first floor, on one side of the huge lobby. The caterers had created a boundary for the room with potted trees strung with white lights. It was so pretty with all the greenery and so cool to have the empty station for our party. Feeling like a teenager, I hid behind the plants until I spotted Nick. He was talking in a group of five people—perfect. God, he looked good in a tux! The event wasn't formal, but wearing a tux was such a Nick thing to do. I should have expected no less. I'm sure he knew what it did for him, not that he needed anything to enhance his looks.

I smoothed my dress, took a deep breath, and went in. I headed straight for Nick. My heart raced, and I could feel my hands start to shake. If this didn't work, I'd be humiliated. When I reached his group, I took his arm and interrupted, "Mind if I steal him for a minute?" He didn't resist. I led him a few steps away, stood on tiptoes, threw my arms around his neck, and kissed him. He kissed back—how I missed those lips! He reached for the small of my back and pulled me close. I leaned my whole body against his as we kissed, right there in front of everyone.

I pulled back and looked deep into those green eyes. "I love you. And I'm so sorry." My eyes filled with tears.

His eyes were already full. "I love you, too, Angie. I'm glad we got that straight. And I'm sorry I got so mad."

"You were right to get mad. I—"

He kissed me again. I was sure people were watching, but that was the point, wasn't it? It felt like a long time to be kissing in public, but I didn't care. I was just happy to be kissing Nick again. After a while, though, I think we both got self-conscious, because we pulled away at the same time. He hugged me, and I put my head on his shoulder.

He whispered in my ear, "I missed you."

I started to tear up again. "I missed you too."

"I think we have to go mingle."

I pulled away. "Yeah, we do."

"Let's get a drink first. What do you want?"

"Sparkling wine."

"Be right back."

Digging in my purse for tissues, I watched him walk away. That ass! I couldn't wait to squeeze it again. When he got back, he handed me my drink and grabbed my hand. We walked over to a group of five people. Sharon Burke was one of them. They drew us into the conversation, and when the subject was exhausted, Sharon asked, "So, you two? How long have you been seeing each other?"

Nick smiled. "About a month."

"Really? Well, I'm happy for you."

I said, "Thanks; we are too." Nick's fingers tightened on my hand.

We wandered over to Melissa's group. The first chance she got, she said, "How long have you been dating?"

I shook my head. "Shut up, Melissa. He knows you know."

She grinned. "Well, I'm glad you're back together. Hey, Nick, this is my fiancé, Jason."

Melissa and I and the guys chatted before we moved on. Nick and I flitted around the reception. Nick was right about our people. No one seemed to judge. With the exception of a couple of young women who'd had their eyes on Nick, everyone seemed happy for us. Nick surprised me when he whispered that one of the guys wasn't too happy that I was taken, either. Really? Who knew?

As Nick and I worked the room, I started to think about what would happen later. I'd never been one for makeup sex, because making up emotionally and having sex were two very different things to me, but Nick and I had been separated for a while, and I was ready to get back to action.

Nick read my mind—either that or he got a hard-on—because he leaned over and whispered in my ear, "Let's get out of here."

I nodded, and we bowed out of the group we were in. We hit the bathrooms on the way out, and when I got out, Nick was waiting for me. He took my shoulders, backed me into the wall, and pressed his body against me. Yep, he had a hard-on. He kissed me like he couldn't get enough. "I can't wait to get you home," he said under his breath.

We walked through the sleeping depot toward the Metro. We made out like teenagers while we waited for our train, and then we graduated to groping once we got on. We got off at Rosslyn and headed to his apartment. There was a man waiting for the elevator when we got there, so we had to cool ourselves off until the fourteenth floor, when he got off. As soon as the doors shut, Nick took my face in his hands and kissed me, backed me against the wall, and pressed his body against mine. From my lips to my pussy, everything ached for more.

When we got into his apartment, we frantically undressed each other, like actors in a movie. He unzipped my dress and helped it fall to the floor. I pushed his jacket off his shoulders and then his suspenders, undid his pants, and let them drop. He unclasped my bra and slid it off, revealing my breasts, nipples at attention.

I struggled to unbutton his shirt as he grabbed my breasts and squeezed, fingers grasping at my nipples. Pleasure shot through me as he caressed them with his thumbs. I was down to the last buttons on his shirt, but I abandoned my quest and reached for his hard-on. I grabbed it through his briefs, and he moaned, knees buckling. He bent down and took my nipple in his mouth, flicking it with his tongue. My lower half tingled, wanting him.

I reached my hand inside his briefs and stroked him. He moaned again. I felt the vibration in my breast. He let go of it and said, "On the floor." He held my hand as I kneeled; then he kneeled and helped me lay down on the rug. I still had panty hose on, and he stroked them and put them against his cheek. "I love the way these feel."

The only thing I could reach was his hair, and I ran my fingers through his soft waves. He hooked his fingers inside my panty hose. "But they've gotta come off." Carefully, he pulled them down and off. He admired my red lace panties. "Oh, that's hot!" He caught the lace in his toothy smile and tugged, eyes playful, reminding me of that first night.

He hooked his thumbs in the sides and pulled my panties off and then took my knees and spread them wide. I helped him, opening to anything he had to offer. His tongue went straight for my clit, licking firm and frantic. I reached for his hands and pulled them up to my breasts. His fingers found my nipples and pinched, pulsing. I moaned. As he licked me, my clit got more and more sensitive until I couldn't take anymore, and I squirted, feeling the pleasure rock my body. He put two fingers in me and pulsed them inside me. "Just like old times."

I laughed and pushed into his fingers. "Fuck me," I said, pushing my breasts together, "up here." He pulled his fingers out. I still wanted them, but I wanted to pleasure him. He straddled me, moving up to align with my breasts. I opened my cleavage for him, and he laid his dick between my breasts. I pushed them tight around him, and he pumped, enjoying the view of the head peeking out the top.

"I love your tits," he said. I pushed them a little tighter. "Oh, you feel so good!" He kept thrusting and then pulled out. "I gotta be inside you." He went for his wallet and looked in it. "Shit. I'll be right back." He got up and headed for the bedroom. I loved seeing his naked ass going and his stiffy coming back. He straddled me and handed me a condom. "Put this on?"

I motioned for him to move up on me, tore the wrapper, and put the tip in my mouth. I grabbed the base of his dick and pushed it toward me while I rolled the condom on with my lips.

He breathed, "I love when you do that." He climbed between my legs, looked up, and said, "Hey, do you wanna do it on the balcony?"

I was so ready for him to plunge into me that it took me a minute to shift gears. "Uh, OK."

He took my hand, helped me up, and led me out to the balcony. He took my waist, turned me away from him, so I faced out, and I held onto the rail and spread my legs. I felt the tip of his dick between my legs, and then it slid into me, filling me up. Nick reached his hands around me and kneaded my breasts as he pumped.

He said into my ear, "I know how you like to be seen." My knees buckled, and he held me up. "Is that someone on the balcony across the street?" He moved his hands to my hips, exposing my breasts. In the dark I couldn't tell if they were looking, but I loved the idea that they could. And I loved the feel of Nick's body against mine, in me, holding onto me.

He reached down to my pubic bone and squeezed the flesh around my clit, igniting the echoes of my last orgasm. He thrust a few more times and then stopped. I heard him strain and felt him twitch as he came inside me. Immediately he moved his hands up to my chest, over my breasts, and hugged me to him. When he let go, I turned around, put my arms around him, and kissed his lips. "That was hot, honey."

Breathing hard, he said, "Let's go back inside."

We went through the sliding glass door, and he led me to the bedroom. He pulled back the covers, and I sat down on the bed.

"I'm gonna go take the condom off," he said, heading to the master bath.

I lay down and left the covers off. I was still hot.

He came out of the bathroom and lay down next to me, pulling me close. "I'm so glad you're back."

I draped one arm around him and laid my head on his shoulder. "Me too."

"I love you."

I snuggled closer. "I love you too."

"I won't let you go again."

"You'd better not."

Epilogue: Six Years Later

"Oh yeah, that's it, right there, right there!" I said as Nick's fingers found the knots in my lower back. I hugged him harder. "Keep going!"

Our son came up and hugged Nick's work pants. "Gwoup hug!"

I put my hand on his back. Nick did the same.

I said, "Hi, sweetie."

Our daughter said, "I'm sweetie. He's honey."

"Sorry. Hi, honey."

"Mommy! I wanna Nutella sandwich!"

"No, honey, it's almost dinnertime."

Our son stamped his foot and whined. "Aw! I wanna sandwich!" He sat on the floor and cried.

Nick whispered in my ear, "Tonight—after they go to bed."

I said, "They've been taking forever to get to sleep."

Nick sighed and whispered, "Dammit, it's been almost a month!"

"I know, honey. Believe me, I know."

He winked. "I'm gonna wake you up in the middle of the night."

Not funny. "No, you won't. I have to sleep. I can't handle them when I'm tired."

His eyes widened. "What do you want me to do?"

"Whatever you need to, hon." He was sweet to save his sexual energy for me, but we got so few chances to consummate that I didn't mind if he jerked off when he needed to.

"Man, remember when we could just do it whenever we wanted to?"

I nodded. "I do remember. And we had the energy."

His eyes narrowed. "What? You don't want to?"

"I'm just tired, honey. Don't take it personally. No mom wants to."

"Mo-om, can I watch TV?" our daughter asked from across the room.

"Mommy's trying to watch the news, honey."

"I'm *sweetie*! Come on, I didn't watch any TV today."

The hell with it. "Fine, change the channel." I went to the sink and filled up the pasta pot.

"What's for dinner?" Nick asked, coming up behind me and holding my waist.

"Spaghetti."

He hugged me. "Remember the first time you made me pasta?"

"Mmmm, that was nice. Remember how I used to make my own gravy?"

Nick sighed again. "*That* was nice."

"I know, honey. Maybe when the kids get a little older, I'll have more time to cook."

"*Mommy*! I gotta go potty!"

I put the pot on the stove, salted it, and turned the burner on. "OK, I'm coming." I headed to the bathroom.

Nick said, "I'm gonna go get undressed."

God! That used to mean something entirely different. Why did we have kids again?

Nick came down and sat in his chair. "Is this today's mail?"

"Yes, it is."

Nick opened an envelope and frowned. "I paid this two months ago. Assholes."

"Language!"

Our daughter yelled, "*Assholes*!"

"Thank you," I said to Nick.

"Sorry," he said. "Honey, we don't use that word."

"I'm *sweetie*!"

He said, "OK, sweetie, we don't use that word."

"Why not?"

"Because it's not a nice word."

"Then why did you use it?"

"Because these people are jerks."

"Then why didn't you say 'jerks'?"

Nick smacked the pile of mail down on the table. "I don't know, sweetie. I don't know."

"Ooo, Panda Princesses' is coming on!" she said.

I finished wiping our son's butt, washed my hands, and motioned to Nick, pointing upstairs and nodding vigorously. I whispered in his ear, "I'll meet you upstairs." I turned and left the room. I got up to the bedroom, took off my clothes, and lay on the bed to wait for him.

About a minute later, he opened the bedroom door, shed his clothes as he walked to the bed, and jumped in next to me. "Finally!" he said as he kissed me. Our tongues played their familiar game, and he reached for second base.

He took my whole breast in his hand, finding the nipple and stroking it. I struggled to get my head in the game, and he broke our kiss to take my other breast in his mouth. He tweaked it with his tongue, but then there was a knock at the door.

"Mommy?" It was our son.

"What, honey?"

"You said you'd make me a Nutella sandwich."

Did I? "Oh shoot. I'll come down in a few minutes, OK."

"But I want my Nutella sandwich!" he whined.

"I don't understand you when you talk like that, honey."

"I want my Nutella sandwich," he said politely. Shit.

I kissed Nick, got up, got dressed, and opened the door. "OK, honey. I'll make your sandwich." If it was good enough for breakfast, it was good enough for dinner.

Nick started to get dressed. The kids weren't allowed to eat without a parent around. Choking was still a big danger at their ages.

I made his sandwich, gave it to him, and looked for a top for the spaghetti pot. Our boy wasn't going to eat dinner, but I was too tired to care and more than a little psyched, because there would be no whining at the table.

After dinner, Nick put on a DVD for the kids and whispered in my ear as I was putting away leftover meatballs, "Meet me upstairs. They're watching a movie."

"OK."

I got the food into the fridge and headed upstairs. The thought of sex was almost palatable, because I'd get to lie down.

I opened the door to the bedroom, and Nick was naked on our four-poster, the royal blue bedding thrown on the floor. He'd puffed out over the years—especially around the middle—but he was still gorgeous to me. And God bless him, he never stopped telling me how beautiful I was, even after two pregnancies. So no matter how I felt, I was gonna do this for him. It wasn't that I wasn't interested in him; it was that the kids leeched all my energy, and after a day with them, I didn't have anything left to give.

I locked the door behind me and took off my juice-stained T-shirt and bra as I approached the bed.

"I love those tits, baby."

I took off my yoga pants and panties. "Mmmm." I climbed on the bed and leaned in for a kiss. He reached for my breast. I remembered the days when it took at least a few kisses to get to second base. I sighed in my head and reached down to grab his hard-on. And it was stiff. When wasn't it? I gave it a tug.

He exhaled, "Oh yeah, baby."

He reached down and stroked my pussy. I moaned, hoping to speed up the process. "I want you in me, baby," I said.

"You don't wanna play?" he asked.

"Let's work on you first, OK?" He always approached sex like it wasn't a race against time, but sadly, that's what it had become.

He extricated his fingers and climbed on top, lined up, and thrust into me. I worked on him, squeezing, breathing hard. His efforts hit a crescendo, and we heard a knock on the door.

"Mommy!"

"What is it, sweetie?" I motioned for Nick to keep pumping.

"The movie stopped."

Shit. "It did? Is it over?"

"No, it's stuck."

Nick slowed down. Shit. "OK, well go down there, and I'll be out in a minute."

"OK."

"Keep going," I whispered.

Nick thrust a few more times, but then he backed out. He shook his head. "I can't finish."

"Oh, honey, can I help?"

"No, it's over."

I felt bad. He looked so disappointed.

"Go fix the kids' movie, honey. I'll be down in a few minutes."

"OK."

I got up, got dressed, and closed the bedroom door. With sad puppy-dog eyes, Nick watched me go.

At bedtime, when our daughter was reading in bed and I was giving our son a bath, Nick poked his head into the bathroom.

"Hon, I've gotta do some work in the bedroom, so I'm letting her read and turn her light out."

He must've gotten a donor e-mail. "OK."

I finished the bath and got the little guy into his jammies, read to him, and cuddled and tucked him in. As I left his room, I noticed that Nick had closed our bedroom door. What kind of work was he doing that he needed privacy?

I opened the door. The lights were dim, and there were flameless candles everywhere—on the heirloom steamer trunk at the foot of the four-poster, on both nightstands, on the end table by the seating area. The candles glowed gold and set off the light-blue walls and royal-blue comforter beautifully. The effort was impressive—Nick had to have gathered all the candles in the house to do this. And the pièce de rèsistance himself was leaning on one elbow, in tight boxer briefs and shirtless, holding a bottle of massage oil.

Tears filled my eyes. "Oh honey, I can't believe you did all this!"

"You seemed a little tense. Come over here and lie down."

I crossed the room, taking off my shirt and bra, and climbed up on the bed and gave him a kiss. "I love you."

"I love you, too," he said. "Now come on, relax."

I lay face down on the bed, and he straddled my thighs. He poured drops of oil on me. I flinched. "Ooh, that's cold!"

"It's about to get warm. Don't worry," he reassured me as he spread the oil over my back. He began to knead my neck.

"Oh yeah, baby." I closed my eyes and savored his firm caresses. His hands moved down to my shoulder blades. "Right in the middle there. That's it." I felt the tension, plus the pain from muscle I'd pulled carrying groceries before he got home, melt away. He kept going, all down my back, and I turned to mush.

He kissed my back. "Are you good?"

"Oh yeah, I'm good," I said. "Thank you. You're so sweet!"

"That's why you love me," he said, dismounting me and lying down beside me. He reached for my cheek, gently turned my head, and gave me a soft kiss. I turned to him, and he put his arm around me, throwing his leg over mine.

We chatted a bit about our day, until I playfully pushed him onto his back.

"What's this?" he asked.

I grinned. "That was just what I needed. Now it's your turn."

He closed his eyes and laid back as I went to work on him.

"I love you, Angie."

"I love you too."

About the Author

J. K. Holiday is a voluptuous woman with a wild past. Since the '90s, she's worked as an obituary writer, energy reporter, freelancer for lifestyle and business magazines, and finally, a fiction writer.

Today she lives in the DC metro area with her two kids. Her hobbies include gardening, cooking, and nature photography. This is her first novel.

CPSIA information can be obtained
at www.ICGtesting.com
Printed in the USA
LVHW021158031021
699374LV00009B/909